BOY

meets

GHOUL

Praise for *Boy meets Hamster*

'A sweet, funny, moving and joyous delight of a novel, full of love and hope, with a great big (giant hamster-sized) heart at its centre.' *Simon James Green*

'A warm, open and generous book with enormous heart . . . genuinly laugh-out-load funny.' *Maggie Harcourt*

'Terrifically comic and diverse . . . A book I wish I could give to teenage me!' *Olly Pike*

'I loved *Boy Meets Hamster*, a fresh, modern LGBTQ+ YA novel about a tale as old as time – that first gay crush!' *The Guyliner*

BIRDIE MILANO

BOY
meets
GHOUL

MACMILLAN CHILDREN'S BOOKS

First published 2019 by Macmillan Children's Books
an imprint of Pan Macmillan
The Smithson, 6 Briset Street, London EC1M 5NR
Associated companies throughout the world
www.panmacmillan.com

ISBN 978-1-5098-4867-6

1 3 5 7 9 8 6 4 2

A CIP catalogue record for this book is available from
the British Library.

Printed and bound by CPI Group (UK) Ltd, Croydon CR0 4YY

For Jo,
I heard you like nice surprises.

ONE

The first time we drove past the front of the stadium, a couple of people turned to give the car a curious look.

By the third time, we'd drawn a bit of a crowd.

The sixth time, there were enough people lining the pavement to make it feel like we were the headline float in a surprise parade. People had their phones out. I wasn't sure if they were filming, or phoning their friends to come and take a look for themselves.

We turned the corner again, and two girls in gym gear dropped their kitbags and stopped dead at the edge of the kerb to stare.

My best friend Kayla cringed and huddled down low in the back seat. 'They look like they've seen a ghost,' she muttered.

I peered out of the window from between my fingers. 'No – just something totally horrific. Have you still got that paper bag we had our lunch in, by the way? I might cut some eyeholes in it and wear it over my head for the rest of my life.'

You wouldn't think there was too much in our car to strike fear into the hearts of the average passer-by. All right, there were enough suitcases piled precariously on top of it to cause a mid-motorway landslide, but for once Mum wasn't driving like she was trying out for Formula One.

I was wearing my Woking FC shirt in the back seat, but it's not like I could have been taken for a football hooligan. After all, I was a bit younger and a lot less drunk and bald than most of the ones you see on the news. I didn't have a flag tattooed across my face or anything.

Kayla looked perfectly respectable with her newly dyed hair gleaming petrol shades of green and blue, and my little brother, Jude, whose bladder was usually a ticking time bomb on any long car journey, was slumped safely snoring against my side, a set of noise-cancelling headphones clamped over his ears.

No. The thing so monstrous it was making people turn and stare as we passed them by – the thing so *embarrassing* that I was willing to put a bag on my head and live the rest of my life pretending to be litter *just* to avoid anyone thinking I was associated with it – wasn't in the back with us at all. It was in the front, relegated to the passenger seat as it'd been too overexcited to drive.

My dad.

Apparently oblivious to the fact that he could take a smack in the face from a lamp post at any minute, he was hanging out of the window like a dog being driven past a sausage factory, bellowing football chants at terrified strangers.

'WOKING ARE MAGIC – IF YOU'RE NOT A FAN, YOU'RE TRAGIC – LALA LA LA – OI! LALA LA LA . . .'

He was flying a massive bath towel with the Woking FC crest on it down the side of the car like a flag, and every so often, he tooted an air horn and yelled, 'WHO-KING? WE-KING! WO-KING!'

Which might not have been a weird thing to see if it had been a match day. Or if he'd been part of a crowd of other noisy, enthusiastic fans. It would definitely have made more sense if we were actually *in* Woking, or if the stadium we were driving past happened to be the setting for an upcoming away game.

But it wasn't. It definitely wasn't.

Because the street we were driving down happened to be the one outside Old Trafford, home of Manchester United, probably the most famous football team in the world. No matter how brilliant Woking were, it was safe to say that they weren't *quite* in the same league. So Dad's enthusiastic support was a bit of a David and Goliath situation.

You know, if David had shown up to fight Goliath by yelling about how awesome he was, on a day when Goliath had gone home to take a nap.

Honestly, I thought Dad might just be overwhelmed by being in such a famous footballing location. Virtually every iconic player must have walked out on to the pitch at Old Trafford at some point. I'd felt a pretty big thrill myself the first time we passed the green glass frontage. I'd only ever seen it on TV before, but now, as we turned to circle the stadium for what seemed like the seven thousandth time, the experience was getting seriously old. And so were Dad's chants:

'TWO-FOUR-SIX, YEAH – THESE WOKING LADS PLAY FOR MANCHES-TER!'

On the pavement, a prim-looking woman almost tripped over her sausage dog as she tried to get away from the noise. I sighed, unwrapping a toffee and holding it out between the seats, in the vain hope he'd take it and stick his teeth together.

'We're not playing *for* Manchester, Dad. We're playing *in* Manchester. There's a difference,' I muttered, eyes rolling so hard I was surprised they stayed in my head.

I hadn't even wanted to come here to begin with. But my half-term plans – my amazing, romantic Halloween hang-out plans – had all fallen apart at the last minute when my new boyfriend, Leo, had cancelled on me. And it turned out that Dad just *happened* to have reserved me a place on a football training camp called Feet of the Future, *just in case*.

It was like he'd been *expecting* my life to fall apart.

My total misery didn't even seem to register with Dad. He was still waving his arms out of the window, narrowly missing swiping the shopping bags off two grans innocently waiting to cross the road.

'Just think,' Dad called back to me, ignoring my sugary bribe, 'in five days, you're going to be playing here!'

I shot a despairing look at Kayla, who now had her head in her hands.

'Not *here* here, Dad. I'm going to be playing on a training pitch somewhere on the other side of the city,' I corrected. 'It's not exactly the start of my Premier League career.'

He blinked at me, then broke into a dopey grin. 'TWO-FOUR-SIX, YAY! MY BOYS WILL MAKE IT BIG SOME DAY!'

The car tyres squealed again as Mum veered off down a side road before Dad could beg her to go round *just one more time*.

Beside me, my little brother wiggled groggily into wakefulness. 'Are we nearly there yet?' he asked, eyes big, brown and watery. 'Because I want to go *home*.'

I couldn't have agreed more. As Old Trafford retreated

into the distance, and I thought about how my dreams of a loved-up Halloween were being crushed under a pair of muddy football boots, all I wanted was to be anywhere but here.

TWO

Sensing Jude gearing himself up to start sobbing, I quickly repurposed the toffee I'd been offering Dad, and shoved it into my brother's mouth instead. Then I slid down as far into my seat as I could and closed my eyes. Maybe if I tried hard enough, I could fall asleep and dream about the way this week was *supposed* to go.

I wasn't meant to spend half-term trapped in a car halfway across the country while Dad tried to think of something clever that rhymed with 'goals'. This week was supposed to be special. It was supposed to be the first real chance I'd had since school started to spend some proper in-person time with my summer-romance-turned-sort-of-boyfriend, Leo.

Closing my eyes made it all too easy to picture him just the way he'd looked on the last day of our trip to Starcross Sands (Cornwall's coolest caravan park). For most of the holiday, he'd been in disguise, playing his part as the park's massive hamster mascot, Nibbles. But during the end-of-season celebrations, he'd thrown off the orange fur and shown up in a white T-shirt and black leather jacket, looking like something out of *Grease*. The disco lights had turned his dark skin different shades of gold and caught the highlights in his eyes perfectly. He'd looked like he was glowing. And when he kissed me, it had felt like I was glowing too.

I could remember it like it was yesterday, not two whole miserable months ago. The way he'd smelt like fairground popcorn when I'd leaned my head against his shoulder. How dancing with him had just felt natural, and not like I was trying to do very hard sums with my feet, like it always had before. How his smile had creased up into dimples at the corner of his mouth, and how he could never say my name without smiling, murmuring it soft and low into my ear, 'Dylan. Dylan.'

'Dylan? Dylan Kershaw, you're pulling kissy faces and saying your own name in your sleep. Consider this fair warning that if you don't wake up now, you're about to become a viral video sensation.'

I blinked one eye open to find Kayla pointing her phone in my direction. I blocked it with the palm of my hand. 'You're evil.'

'I'm saving you from yourself. *And* from myself. The video really is hilarious – want to see?'

Hissing at her, I shook my head and dragged myself upright again. 'I wasn't sleeping. Anyway, why bother? None of my dreams ever work out.'

Kayla twisted her lips together, looking sceptical.

'That seems a little dramatic. Just because you're not getting to see Leo this week?'

'And because every other time I've seen him, something's gone horribly wrong. Like the weekend right after school started, when his parents *and* my parents decided to come along, and the whole date was just us eating the world's most awkward Whoppers while they argued about politics. Then there was the cinema date, when all the good films had sold out, and we ended up watching *Twinkle the Talking Train's Big Journey* surrounded by four-year-olds crying and giving off unsettling odours.'

I looked at Jude, still sucking on his toffee. It hadn't been too different from this car journey, in fact.

Kayla leaned back and held up her hands like she was framing a camera shot. 'Welcome to *Dylan Kershaw's Dating Disasters*. We join almost-fifteen-year-old Dylan as he navigates the rocky terrain of dating his dream boy.' She grinned. 'I think it could be a hit. We'll get Bear Grylls to narrate, and there can be a date where you have to drink your own wee to survive.'

I scowled across at her. 'Has anyone ever told you you're not very funny?'

'No, never,' she said, wide-eyed in fake innocence. 'Everyone thinks I'm hilarious. But, Dylan, all of that stuff's just about the circumstances not being right. It

9

doesn't have anything to do with you and Leo. And he still wants to see you, doesn't he? What happened with this week, anyway? I thought you had plans.'

Silently, I opened the messages screen on my phone and held it up for her to see.

Kayla squinted at it for a moment, then just said, 'Oh.'

We *had* had plans. Leo was going to come and visit me for the first time, and I'd been totally ready to show him the cultural delights of Woking town centre. I'd even ranked all the restaurants in order of most to least romantic, starting with the fancy place in the local manor house and going down to the burger van in the market that was set up a bit too close to the fish stand.

But Leo had suddenly got a real, professional dancing job in a real, professional show, and now he was going to be away for rehearsals the entire week.

Even that should have been fine because, obviously, if you're *really* in love then you shouldn't need to see each other all the time. There are loads of romantic sayings about it, like 'absence makes the heart grow fonder'. And whether Leo is near or far – according to the wisdom of Celine Dion – my heart *will* go on.

So it was weird that, as I stared at the text message on my phone and read **Something's come up**, my heart was feeling less like it was going to *go on*, and more like

10

it had been dropped into a car compactor and squashed thin and flat.

It's not like I expected him to pick seeing me over his dancing. It just might have been nice if he had. Or even if he could have done both. Just one day together would have been better than nothing.

Now I was going to be stuck at football camp for a whole week, pretending I was *fine*. I was trying to be cool about it, but secretly I felt like throwing the world's biggest tantrum.

Though from the siren-blast wailing coming from the seat next to me, it seemed Jude had beaten me to it. Kayla was patiently feeding him toffees, but they only temporarily muffled the din.

'Can't you *stop*?' I asked him, trying to figure out what I'd done with the earbuds for my phone.

'Not going to,' Jude retorted between sugar-sticky sobs. 'Not until we go home.'

'Then it's going to be a very long cry,' I warned him. 'We're staying for a week.'

'He probably just misses Fluffy,' Kayla suggested.

Fluffy. Jude's brand-new pet hamster, bought for him because of his obsession with the character Leo had played at Starcross Sands. Jude had even wanted to name it Nibbles after him, but I had to veto that one quickly. I didn't want my little brother cleaning out the cage of something named after the alter ego of the boy who'd been my first kiss.

We were going to be staying in a hotel with a NO PETS policy, so Jude had been forced to leave Fluffy in the care of our gran. He'd kicked up quite a fuss.

'Fluffy hasn't gone anywhere,' Kayla said, rubbing Jude's back in what looked like a reassuring way. 'He's just stayed at home.'

'But I *love him*,' Jude wailed, his sobs getting back into glass-shattering territory. 'I love him and want him with me *all the time*.'

Kayla and I shared a mutual eye-roll. All out of toffees, I put in my earbuds and cranked up the Deathsplash Nightmares' screamiest hit.

Jude was being ridiculous, which was fair enough really, since he was only five.

The problem was, I was starting to think I knew exactly how he felt.

THREE

It turned out even heavy metal couldn't compete with Jude's decibel level. I was *trying* to brood over my tragic lack-of-love life but kept getting interrupted by a wail of 'WANT HOME, WANT MY HOUSE, WANT HOOOOOME'. I wasn't sure exactly at what age it stopped being socially acceptable to just yell out anything you fancied, whenever you fancied it, but if I could have joined in by wailing 'WANT LEO, WANT PIZZA, WANT A SOCIAL LIFE NOT TOTALLY PLANNED BY MY PARENTS' and got away with it, then I probably would have.

'What are you doing to my littlest boy?' Mum asked, peering over her shoulder when we stopped at the lights. Somehow, she managed to keep her voice at a normal level while still cutting through his din.

'We're not doing anything!' I said. 'He's protesting about being kidnapped – you did teach him to shout if anyone tried to take him somewhere he didn't want to go.'

I wasn't sure it counted as kidnapping when it was your own kid, but Jude might not have grasped the complexities of that, yet.

'He's purple.' Mum pursed her lips. 'That's not a normal colour for a child to go. Not *blueberry*-purple.'

I helped Jude to sit upright again, surreptitiously checking he wasn't choking on a toffee. He *was* looking a bit swollen and fruity.

'He's in mourning,' Kayla said, as Mum turned back to the road.

Dad was still trying to catch a last glimpse of the football stadium, ignoring us, with his backside wiggling hideously as he leaned out of the window.

'He can't be in mourning,' I argued. 'Fluffy's not dead; he's just been left at home.'

This prompted another hiccupy sob from Jude.

'Yes, but he *could* be dead,' Kayla retorted, triggering another, much louder sob. 'It's like Schrödinger's hamster.'

'No,' I said. 'It's Jude's hamster – that's the whole point.'

Kayla tutted at me and went on. 'Schrödinger was this physicist who said that if you put a cat in a box, once the lid was closed, you couldn't know for sure whether the cat was alive or dead until you opened it again.'

'What does that have to do with hamsters?'

'It's not about the hamster – it's about whether or not it's dead.'

14

I clamped my hands tightly over my ears as Jude dutifully let off a mammoth wail. He was turning raspberry-red now. At this rate, he'd have worked through all the shades of the fruit bowl before we got to where we were staying.

'Nobody's dead,' Mum cut in sharply from the front. 'Now drop it, you two.'

Even though she wasn't looking at us, the tone of voice she used made both Kayla and me nod sheepishly.

Dad slid back through the window and turned round in his seat with a dramatic flourish.

'Jude, we'll call Gran and have her put Fluffy on Skype later. Right, are we nearly there yet?'

I couldn't believe Dad had been bouncing in his seat the whole way and was *still* using that line.

'We are indeed . . . In fact –' Mum smiled smugly across at him and threw the car expertly into a parking space – 'we're here.'

The spot Mum had picked sat in the shadows of a massive black bus, but everything else around us was gleaming brightly in the reflected glow from the huge silver building towering over the car park.

'That's the hotel?' I gripped the edge of Dad's seat with both hands and knelt forward to get a better look. It was completely out of place, like aliens had touched down in a massive shiny spaceship then forgotten where they'd parked it and caught a taxi home.

'That's the one.' Dad nodded, turning off his *Best of Queen* CD. 'Nothing but the best for the feet of the future.'

It really did look like it had fallen from outer space. A giant silver cosmic needle stuck right in the middle of an ordinary brick city. It must have had a hundred floors, each with its own shimmering window looking down at us.

We'd never stayed anywhere bigger than a Travelodge before.

It was the kind of place you'd put on tourist posters. A Landmark hotel. The kind of place that . . .

I reached over and clutched at Kayla's shoulder.

'Look at it! It's the kind of place you'd go for a *dream holiday*.'

Kayla didn't reply. I assumed she was basking in the reflected silvery glory of us finally getting to live our best lives, but when I glanced across, she wasn't even looking in the right direction.

Instead, she was staring, transfixed, at the glossy black side of the bus beside us.

'We've got to get out of here,' she said, finally, as Mum hauled Jude out of the car to shake him down for crumbs and squashed toffees.

'We *are* getting out,' I said. 'Obviously. Did you think

16

we were just going to look at the giant, amazing alien hotel across the road and then sleep on the back seat of the car?'

I had a moment's panic that Dad might yank a tent out of the boot and announce that car-park camping was actually the plan. But he and Mum were starting to unpack our bags and get Jude into his wheelchair. This was really about to be real.

Kayla was shaking, and it didn't seem to be from excitement. 'No, Dylan – we've got to get out of here. Right. Now.'

She started grabbing her things frantically, piling magazines into her bag and throwing the Travel Scrabble board in on top so that SKITTLES (twelve points) and PUSTULES (triple-word score) scattered everywhere. Then she climbed straight into my lap and tugged on the handle of the door on my side.

'What are you *doing*?' I spluttered. 'You can't just run off into the wilds of Manchester. You don't know what's out there.'

Neither did I, except for two football clubs and some wild, shouty bands my dad liked. But that still didn't mean Kayla should be in the middle of it on her own.

'I do know what's *out there*, Dylan.' Kayla got one leg out of the car and tried to hop away while I held her back by the other ankle. She'd pulled her jacket up over her head like a paparazzi-shy celebrity. 'And I can't let them see me like this. I'm not ready.'

She got down on to her knees and started crawling alongside the car with her bag clutched to her stomach like a stealthy upside-down tortoise. I slowly climbed out to see what she'd been looking at. It was just a bus. The giant silver space hotel probably had a lot of coach trips coming through.

But, as I straightened up, I realized how wrong I was. It wasn't *just* a bus at all. It had a logo on its side, and it didn't look like the kind of thing Sunny Dayz Coach Holidays would think of as on-brand.

It was a skull.

A huge, grinning skull covering half of the upper deck. Around it hung a shower of glittering raindrops, picked out in what looked like actual crystals. Along the side, they clustered together to form words.

'*Now* do you see?' Kayla hissed from her hiding place.

I did. I couldn't exactly *help* seeing, what with it being spelled out in sparkly letters six feet above my head. Feet of the Future might have been the reason Dad had brought *me* to Manchester this week, but Kayla hadn't come along to get her trainers dirty.

In fact, she'd been trying to figure out how to get to Manchester this particular week for months. My dad's secret football-camp plans had come at just the right

18

time for her – she'd signed up for Feet of the Future's associated cheer squad immediately and talked my parents into bringing her along with us.

But it wasn't really about cheerleading at all. The *real* reason Kayla wanted to come was that the Deathsplash Nightmares were playing a concert at Old Trafford on the last day of the camp.

Tickets had sold out in seconds. After all, they only played one UK date each year. But Kayla wasn't going to let a little thing like tickets stop her. She'd come to Manchester to find a way to see her favourite band.

And it looked like she'd found one.

She just clearly hadn't expected to be parked right next to them when she had a stray toffee squished into her baggy car clothes, and she hadn't even bothered to do her hair.

'Look, Kayla!' Mum announced, oblivious to the series of panic attacks my best friend was having on the car park tarmac. 'Aren't they that pop group you like?'

Kayla made a small strangled noise and started to drag herself away across the ground. I could tell she wasn't herself, because if she had been, she'd have told Mum that they weren't a *pop group*, they were the *best metal band in the world*. And that she didn't *like* them – her fandom was the truest, purest form of devotion humans were capable of. And that yes – *obviously* – it was them. Just in case anyone wasn't clued in by the skull and water droplets, they'd helpfully spelled it out in metre-high letters, which Mum sounded out slowly, as if she were reading a foreign language: 'THE DEATHSPLASH NIGHTMARES'.

FOUR

The Nightmares weren't actually *on* the bus, obviously. Even Kayla had to admit that the world's greatest metal band probably weren't going to be spending their time prepping for the big Ghoulish Games gig by hanging out in the local car park.

They were staying in our hotel, though.

As we got closer to the silver space needle – Kayla swaying slightly on still-shaky limbs – we started to notice a crowd around the entrance to the lobby. It was made up of teenagers in Deathsplash T-shirts, clustered blackly together like a low-hanging storm cloud. We watched while a young family tried to get out of the lobby doors, pushing through the tangle of pale, lanky limbs. Some of the more hardcore fans peered suspiciously into their pram, just in case Rick Deathsplash was hiding in there as part of a clever undercover ruse, sucking on a dummy and trying to look discrete.

'Do you think they're *all* here for the contest?' Kayla asked, sounding slightly overwhelmed.

The Ghoulish Games concert itself wasn't until Halloween, in five days' time. But Kayla had found out about a competition the local radio station was running.

Calling on fans to show who was the 'coolest ghoul', it was going to involve a series of challenges, ending in a live final to find the biggest Deathsplash superfan. The winner would get two VIP tickets to Old Trafford for the concert: it was the only way Kayla would have a chance to go. The part of the prize she was most excited about involved getting to meet the band afterwards. She was hoping to stand close enough to be flicked with some of Rick's hair sweat.

If her dad had been here, he wouldn't have let her enter the contest. She'd been trying to make him a Deathsplash fan too, but repeated exposure to songs like 'Graveyard Gyrations' and 'Werewolf in Wonderland' had only left him convinced that the Deathsplash Nightmares were some undercover cult, trying to lure in innocent teenagers through loud noises and occasionally rhyming lyrics. But Kayla's dad was at home with a crippling case of man-flu, and my parents were way more easily distracted. We'd thought we just might be able to do it.

Kayla was right, though. Judging by the fans stalking the hotel, there was going to be *a lot* of competition.

'Look on the bright side,' I suggested, as we elbowed our way through the superfans and into the lobby. 'We're in the same hotel as Deathsplash now. If you don't win those tickets, at least you might get up close and personal with them over the breakfast buffet.'

'Rock stars don't *do* buffets,' Kayla countered. 'They have personal chefs to cook them tailored macrobiotic meals. I read that Jenna Deathsplash will only eat from plates containing something hot, something sweet, something crunchy and something blue.'

'I thought that was the list of what brides wear to their weddings,' I said, as she let out an exasperated sigh. 'All right, maybe not something crunchy. Anyway, they can't *all* be here for the concert. Some of them are probably football fans too.'

She sighed mournfully. 'I don't think so, Dylan. Why would you think that?'

I nudged Kayla until she looked in the same direction I was.

'I just have a hunch.' I grinned. 'A sneaking suspicion. I think I might be some kind of psychic, actually.' I nodded my head towards the foyer.

There, standing in front of the check-in desk, was a couple about my parents' age. Saying they looked like Manchester United fans was like saying that water was a little bit wet. They were both wearing red, black and gold scarves that read *MANCHESTER FOREVER*, and jackets with the United crest embroidered on to the back. The man had a cap with the same logo and a red woolly wig sewn under it. A huge flag trailed from one of their bags.

'And there isn't even a match on today,' I whispered to Kayla. 'This must be their casual, everyday look.'

Turning to point them out to my parents, I saw Dad standing frozen behind Jude's chair. He already had the pair fixed with a glare hard enough to punch a hole in concrete. I groaned, because I knew exactly what he was thinking:

Challenge accepted.

When it came to football, Dad considered himself a cut above other, less dedicated, fans. He'd even got me kicked off the school football team by being too enthusiastic on the sidelines (although that was less down to his homemade banners and chants, and more because he'd started picking fights with the ref). At Woking FC matches, he was usually the only person with his face painted in the team's colours, and he'd run down the side of the pitch with a flag even when they didn't win. Dad *loved* a competition.

I just hoped the poor strangers at the desk were getting out of the hotel today, before Dad could turn them into his unwitting arch nemeses.

Or maybe they wouldn't have to.

As Kayla and I watched, Dad left Mum to look after Jude and the bags and made a mad dash towards the toilets. With any luck, it was a sudden bout of food poisoning – something bad enough to put him off getting into any weird fan wars with complete strangers.

Mum was rummaging through her bag for the things we needed to check in, when out of the corner of my eye, I noticed someone acting strangely. A tall boy with pale copper curls and his jacket collar pulled up so high it hid most of his face was edging across the hotel lobby to join the football-mad pair at the desk. They had to be his parents. I recognized his hunched-over posture as the same one I adopted when I was out with Dad on match days. A combination of trying to be as inconspicuous as possible and hoping that the ground might be kind enough to open up and swallow you whole. There never seemed to be a sinkhole around when you needed one.

But I recognized something else too. A few somethings, as it happens. That hair, for one thing: the perfect autumn-leaf combination of orange and gold. Even though his current posture made him look like he was auditioning for the main part in *The Hunchback of Notre Dame*, I could tell that when he straightened up, he'd be broad-shouldered and athletic.

With perfect, straight white teeth, and skin that had never heard of acne.

And a laugh I could pick out from a hundred different crowds.

All right, some of that wasn't what I *recognized* – it was just what I knew.

Because I knew the boy by the desk. Way, way better than I'd like.

Kayla was a few seconds behind me, but she spotted him too. 'Isn't that –?

I swallowed down the sudden nervous lump in my throat and nodded. 'Mm-hmm.'

'What's *he* doing here?' she whispered urgently.

He was my first big crush. Freddie Alton, sports captain at our school. Freddie of the perfect hair, perfect face, and perfect penalty score. Freddie Alton, who I'd never managed to say a whole word to, despite having known and fancied him since I was twelve. Not that *he* knew that. Whenever *he* was around, all the words dried up on my tongue. Trying to get a sentence out was like hunting for a vowel oasis in an endless vocabulary desert.

You see, I had this old habit of finding it hard to talk to people I had crushes on. I thought meeting Leo had cured it, but *this* crush was different. This was *Freddie*.

Freddie who, I was rapidly figuring out, must also

26

have been booked on to the Feet of the Future week by his own football-mad dad.

Kayla nudged me. 'Well, if nothing else, at least you're not going to have the most embarrassing parent on the sidelines this time.'

There was that small olive branch of mercy. I thanked every lucky star I could think of that Dad seemed to have moved into the hotel loos permanently, so he couldn't show me up for once. And that's when I heard it.

'TWO-FOUR-SIX, YEAH – MY BOYS ARE PLAYING FOR MANCHES-TER!'

At the front desk, Freddie and his parents looked up, looked at me, and then looked over to where Dad was emerging from the bathrooms in his head-to-toe brand-new look.

FIVE

Unbeknown to any of us, Dad had splashed out on a whole new kit for this trip. Gone was his old, so-threadbare-it-was-almost-translucent, 70s strip, to be replaced with a brand-new set in Woking FC's colours, with the shirt customized to read *Kickin' Kershaw* on the back.

Which was great, because now if anyone wondered whether it was me, Dylan Kershaw, who had the most embarrassing dad in the world, they'd have a handy visual clue.

And if they had doubts about just *how* embarrassing Dad was, they'd be able to tell by the way he still thought you could make words 'cool' by leaving off the *g* at the end.

Kickin'.

Playin'.

Stylin'.

Slowly dyin' of total mortification.

I could see Freddie Alton gradually regaining his composure as I lost mine. It was fine to have cringeworthy parents, just so long as they weren't the worst in the room.

His parents had come dressed as the window display in the Manchester United tourist shop. *My* dad had gone one step further. He was wearing two giant foam hands, with which he was doing a triumphant pointy dance to punctuate his chants. One of the hands read *DYLAN* across the palm. The other read *JUDE*. He had a massive scarf draped over his shoulders, big enough to hold up and use as a banner. I could just about make out that it said *KERSHAW BOYS SCORE FOR GLORY*.

I didn't know about the other Kershaw boy – Jude was looking pretty delighted by Dad's attempt at outdoing a cheerleader, but he could barely read, so he couldn't possibly understand the true horror. Meanwhile, I was feeling about as unglorious as I ever had.

Dad was eyeballing Freddie Alton's parents like he was daring them to one-up *this*.

Freddie's parents narrowed their eyes right back.

I didn't even want to look at Freddie's reaction, but somehow his flawless face caught my attention anyway, and I was surprised to see something other than total, mocking humiliation there. It almost looked like he understood.

Like a cowboy in a Western as the clock ticks round to high noon, Dad sauntered towards the desk.

The rest of the lobby turned slowly to see how

Freddie's dad would respond to this intrusion on his superfan territory. Women clutched their children closer. The girl behind the desk shivered in fear.

Freddie's dad lifted his chin, folded his arms, and got nudged firmly out of the way by Freddie's mum, who stepped forward to face Dad head-on.

I knew what the look in her eyes was saying as soon as I saw it: *Challenge accepted.*

'Dylan, darling, get Kayla's bags and go and wait by the exit, please. Once we've checked in, we can go and find our room in the outbuilding.'

Mum barrelled into me, on a mission to stand Dad down before tensions escalated and a two-person football riot broke out in the lobby of our gleaming, cosmic hotel. But what she was saying didn't quite make sense.

'The exit?' Kayla asked.

At the same time, I was asking, 'The outbuilding?'

'Yes.' Mum tutted impatiently. 'Didn't you see it on the other side of the car park? That's where Feet of the Future are putting us up. It's all self-catering, of course – communal bathrooms, that kind of thing. This place just handles the keys. You didn't think we'd be in the main hotel, did you? The prices must be astronomical. The rooms probably come with their own linen!'

Mum's preferred holiday destinations were usually caravan parks, where you paid as few pounds as possible to bring your own food and bedsheets and made your own fun. She'd never understood that I wanted to have fun made *for me*, just once. Or at least a bed made for me in the morning, using sheets that didn't have racing cars printed on them and that I hadn't used since I was five.

I gave Kayla a mournful look. My dreams of staying in the silver space needle had just fallen to earth with a crash. I was too depressed to even try to croak out a hello to Freddie, though I was sure I saw him look over as his parents ushered him past us, making swiftly for the same doors. His mum was obviously already plotting the outfit upgrades she'd need to outdo Dad.

Miserably, I trailed over to where Jude and Kayla's three pink suitcases were waiting. Each case was about as big as my brother's powerchair.

'We're staying in the outbuilding,' I told Jude.

'Outside the building?' he asked, looking suddenly distraught. 'But I'll be cold!'

'We're staying *in* a building *called* an outbuilding,' Kayla explained, catching up with me.

She pointed at the glass doors, where we could just see a squat red-brick square sitting huddled on the other side of the car park. It didn't gleam space-age silver. It didn't gleam at all. It just sat there, dull and unimpressive, behind the gang of Deathsplash fans with their faces pressed to the lobby windows.

Kayla sighed. 'It must be some sort of overflow building for the hotel.'

'Yeah, like a *drain* overflow,' I said glumly.

'Don't be such a wet wipe,' Kayla clucked. 'If it's good enough for Freddie—'

'You're just relieved you don't have to come up with something cool to say if you run into the Deathsplashes getting cornflakes,' I snapped.

'I told you, rock stars don't eat cornflakes,' she said. 'Although I suppose they could count as something crunchy.'

I tuned her out. It wasn't *just* that I'd been robbed of my fantasies of staying in the world's fanciest hotel. That was totally rubbish, of course, but not the real problem. The real problem was that Freddie Alton was going to be even more unavoidable if we were staying in the same small hallway.

Maybe if we just met at the football camp I could pretend I was someone gruff and aloof who was too focused on his game to have much to say. But what if we ended up in adjoining rooms? I wouldn't be able to open the door without spending twenty minutes working out my outfit choices and gelling my hair.

There were a thousand and one reasons I shouldn't even be thinking about Freddie.

1. He was with his parents.
2. I was with my *criminally embarrassing* parents.
3. That combination was enough to mark me out as a social pariah before I'd even said hello.
4. Not that I *could* say hello, because as soon as he looked at me, I wouldn't even be able to talk – meaning there was no chance we'd suddenly become friends, let alone anything else.
5. Not that I was interested in anything else!
6. Because I had a boyfriend.
7. Or a sort-of boyfriend, which is nearly the same thing.
8. And Leo probably wasn't really trying to break up with me by never being around.
9. So there was no point even thinking about talking to Freddie.
10. Although technically you could kiss someone without talking to them at all.
11. Though I didn't want to kiss him either!
12. Even if he did have a *really nice mouth* . . .

*

Kayla hissed, '*Dylan*,' and kicked me in the ankle before I realized I'd said that last one out loud. She was glaring daggers at me.

'What?' I stuttered. 'I was thinking about . . . football?'

'Football?' she said, flatly disbelieving.

'I was! Goals . . . have mouths. Mouth of the goal. I was thinking about pitch design. It's a technical term. You wouldn't understand.' I was pretty sure I'd dug myself out of that hole expertly, but Kayla was still looking dubious.

'Just make sure you keep your foot out of your really nice mouth this week, Dylan – OK? And keep away from anyone else's. Leo's worth wait—'

'Boys, Kayla!' Mum interrupted from halfway across the lobby. 'You'd better come over here.'

She and Dad were standing shoulder to shoulder next to a lady in a sharply tailored, official-looking suit. All three of them wore grim expressions.

Mum folded her arms and waited for me to wheel all three of Kayla's cases across in a convoy before continuing, 'There's been a terrible problem with the booking. They haven't got our rooms.'

SIX

Immediately my mind flooded with relief. They didn't have our rooms! Now we could go home, and I could spend the week pining for Leo somewhere private, like under the duvet, listening to all the songs I'd decided would be 'ours' once I had the chance to play them to him. Maybe I could even beg Dad (after he'd healed his broken heart and found out whether they accepted returns on customized football kit) to take me to meet Leo after a rehearsal.

Or, if we had to stay in Manchester, maybe we'd be forced to book into a proper hotel now. Somewhere with its own linen.

Immediately, a worse thought struck me. There weren't any caravan parks near Old Trafford, were there?

The manager with my parents cleared her throat. 'The rooms originally booked are not available, no. We do have *a* room, which we'd like to offer.'

My heart wasn't sure whether to lift or sink. Why was everyone looking so distressed if all the hotel was doing was moving us a bit further down the hall?

'*A* room,' Mum repeated, in the same tone of voice

she'd use to say *a dungheap*. 'Which, if I understand correctly, Ms Toshkhani, you expect the five of us to share.'

Kayla and I exchanged looks. That sounded way too close for comfort.

Folding her arms, Ms Toshkhani met Mum's disapproving look head-on. Most people had trouble making eye contact with Mum when she was angry. She could fell a grown man with a glare. Her blinks were like bullets.

'Unfortunately, as I explained, the accessible floor of our outbuilding has experienced some . . . pest-control issues.'

'They've got rats,' Dad whispered, deafeningly loud.

'The matter is being taken care of,' the manager went on, cutting him off before his 'subtle' comments sent anybody out screaming. 'However, we've had to reallocate any bookings made in association with the wheelchair football group.'

That was Whizzy Wheels, the kids club Jude was meant to attend while I was at Feet of the Future, and which Dad was treating like a training ground for elite Paralympic athletes.

'We have a limited number of accessible rooms within this hotel, and they are all now allocated,' Ms Toshkhani said. 'Except one. One of our suites. That's what we would like to offer to you today.'

'To *share*,' Mum reminded her.

'Yes – but it does have three rooms,' Dad put in, helpfully. 'That's one more than we actually booked.'

We were being moved to a suite with *three* bedrooms? I shot a disbelieving glance at Kayla. 'They have *suites* in the outbuilding?'

'No,' Ms Toshkhani said, offering me a small smile. 'But we have several on the penthouse floor of this hotel. In addition to the bedrooms, you'll also find an accessible wet room, a living room with home-cinema facilities and a small kitchenette.'

Mum looked dangerously like she was about to turn down the offer, all because it came with only one room number.

'Mum, that's bigger than anything you'd get at a caravan park.' I staged my counter-protest before she could. 'And I bet the home-cinema facilities have more than three working TV channels and one fuzzy one where you can occasionally hear somebody reading the news. Right?'

Ms Toshkhani nodded. 'You'll have full access to all the subscription channels, including film and sport.'

'Sport . . .' Dad murmured softly, and I could tell he was sold.

Mum still seemed to be wavering.

'Ms Toshkhani,' came Kayla's voice from behind me. It was the special tone she used for talking to adults she wanted to impress. The one that made her sound exactly like them. She called it her *lawyer voice*: just one of the tools that would make her a success in her dazzling future legal career. 'I think we can all agree that this is a generous offer, in the light of our *preferred* accommodation becoming unavailable. Just one question, regarding bedding. If we prefer, would it be acceptable to use our own linen?'

A sudden light shone in Mum's eyes.

Ms Toshkhani blinked a little but managed not to look too confused as she nodded. 'If that's your preference, then of course, that's quite all right.'

Mum stuck out a hand to shake. 'Then we accept. On *this* occasion.'

As if we got offered budget-price stays in luxury suites at mega hotels all the time. Mum probably avoided even strolling past the Ritz in London for fear of a concierge running out and begging her to take a room. If they did, she'd probably only accept on the condition that she could fill the fridge with supermarket closing-hour-discount sandwiches.

The penthouse floor even *smelt* expensive. Like the perfume hall of a department store, but without assistants trying to spray things in your face. A gentle waft of something fragrant drifted down a hallway where the floors looked like marble, the wallpaper swirled with silver designs, and little tables holding vases of flowers had been placed into alcoves. I wanted to rub my thumb over a petal to check if they were real.

And I probably would have if we weren't being followed by two porters – one pushing all our stuff, the other dragging Kayla's.

'What have you actually got in those cases?' I asked her, while Dad pulled out the key card we'd been given for our room and showily swiped it in the doorway. Then turned it around so that the magnetic strip actually faced the lock and swiped it again.

'Oh, just the essentials,' Kayla replied breezily. 'Oh my . . .'

'What?' I asked, just as I turned my head to see the door swinging open. 'Oh my *God*.'

The suite was *huge*. When I'd told Mum it sounded bigger than the caravans we usually stayed in, I hadn't realized you'd be able to park at least two of them in the living room alone.

Everything was cream, from the polished floors to the heavy, draped curtains, except for one wall, which was set with a huge black screen almost as big as you'd get at the local Odeon. Arty prints featuring cryptic-looking paint splodges hung on the walls. The sofa was a huge letter *L* big enough for all of us to sit on at once, and the windows were six feet high and doubled as a door on to the balcony.

In short, the room was totally *amazing*. It was dripping with so much luxury, it looked like a Kardashian had exploded all over it.

The bedrooms were amazing too. Kayla had made us pick before we went inside, just in case we ended up in a vicious legal dispute over who had the better view and comfier cushions, but they turned out to be an identical mix of white sheets (Mum wasn't getting *near* my bed with her decrepit cotton racing cars – I didn't care if they'd been my favourites when I was five) and floor-to-ceiling views over the city.

I hadn't seen much of Manchester yet, but it was pretty beautiful from this angle. I could see the splay of rooftops in a way most people never get to, unless they happen to be a superhero and are contractually obliged to spend most of their time either brooding on one or leaping from building to building. Even the pigeons looked pretty from this high up.

Mum and Dad delivered a stern lecture that the first rule of the minibar was that nothing ever left the minibar (not even the M&Ms, not even if we were starving, not even in the event of a nuclear apocalypse when all other food was rendered radioactive). Dad was convinced they had spy cameras adding an extra fifty quid to the room bill every time someone so much as looked hopefully at a bottle of Perrier.

After we promised not to even think about snagging a pricy snack, they headed back down to the car for the Rollator walker, which Jude could use instead of his chair around the hotel, and a few extra bags.

Everything was peaceful. Serene. I looked around, and it was like this was exactly where I'd been meant to be all my life. Somewhere with soundproofed windows and piped muzak tinkling gently in the hallway. Somewhere I could take amazing photos for social media.

I whipped out my phone to take one as I thought of it. Kayla was already livestreaming a full room tour to her dad.

Inside the little square of my screen, the room looked perfect: sofa, deep and comfy; the huge TV, gleaming and bright. And my little brother, silhouetted in the doorway of the main bedroom, holding a cardboard box upside down over his lap . . . and looking completely horrified.

I blinked up from my phone as Jude started yelling, 'He's gone! He's *gone*. Shroodimmer ate my hamster!'

SEVEN

'Who did *what*?' I said, rushing across to Jude and almost colliding with Kayla doing the same thing.

'*What* did Schrödinger do?' she asked.

'Shroodimmer ate my hamster!' Jude wailed again.

'But Fluffy's at home with Gran, being overfed carrots and having his fur set in curlers at night.'

'No, he's s'posed to be here – I put him in this box!' Jude waved the evidence at me. 'And when I opened it to make sure he wasn't dead, he wasn't there at ALL.'

Giving me a grim look, Kayla edged past Jude into the bedroom. We both knew what this meant. Jude had smuggled Fluffy along for the ride, and somehow the little creature had made a break for it when Mum and Dad had unpacked the car.

The hamster would be halfway across Manchester by now. I hoped the northern rodents wouldn't give our soft southern one a hard time. I also hoped we'd be able to find a local pet shop stocking orange hamsters with little smudges of white on their noses, or we'd be in a lot of trouble.

Poor Fluffy.

Trying to look positive, I crouched down next to Jude. 'Don't worry – nothing's eaten him. That thing Kayla said about Schrödinger's cat was just nonsense.'

'It was a thought experiment!' Kayla called back.

'Exactly,' I said. 'So you don't need to think about it. Fluffy's just gone to do . . . whatever hamsters do for fun when they're on holiday. Taking tours of people's allotments, getting to know the local mice. I'm sure he's fine—'

'Or he might not be,' Kayla's voice cut in.

I could have murdered her; I'd almost got Jude to calm down.

'I'm sure he *is*,' I called back. 'Almost a thousand per cent sure.'

Jude looked back and forth between us, moving his chair back into the room to stare at Kayla where she stood beside the bed. I followed him in.

'Well, you'd be almost a thousand per cent *wrong*,' she told me, gesturing to the pile of clothes on my parents' bed. 'About Fluffy being off sightseeing, anyway. The only sight he's seen so far is the inside of Jude's pants. Can you pass me that box?'

That's when I saw it. A pair of *Twinkle the Talking Train* underpants was creeping slowly and silently along the side of the bed.

43

'FLUFFY!' Jude yelped delightedly.

I hurriedly threw Kayla the box and ran to crouch down in front of the runaway underwear. Kayla approached from behind. Slowly, carefully she lowered the box over the pants.

They dashed away.

Unprepared, I yelped and fell over as the hamster-powered pants rampaged towards me.

'Dylan!' Kayla yelled, climbing over me and aiming for the underwear again.

She slammed the box down, just missing the speeding pants as they turned in a skidding circle towards the door. I grabbed a shopping bag and gave chase too. We almost got Fluffy in the living room, as the pants tore across the couch, before he finally emerged through a leg hole and flung himself down into the furry rug.

First, Kayla tried to drop the box over him.

Then I nearly scooped him into my bag.

Finally, right by the suite door, Kayla threw the box to me and tossed herself down on the floor as a human barrier. With one last, desperate effort, I dropped the box and managed to trap the fuzzy little speed demon.

We lay there, gasping at our own success.

Until the door opened, abruptly knocking the box over as Mum and Dad staggered through it with Jude's walker and a collection of other bags.

Behind them, a streak of orange disappeared at warp speed down the hallway.

'MY HAMSTER!' Jude wailed. 'I LOST MY HAMSTER!'

Looking up from where I lay, despairing, I noticed an uncharacteristically anxious twitch tug at the corner of Mum's mouth before she replied.

'Not this again, sweetheart. We've just had a call from Gran, and she says Fluffy's *fine*.'

'They're having a great time together,' Dad added quickly. 'Eating salads. Watching soaps.'

Kayla looked at me. I gave her a mystified shrug in return.

Jude was looking more confused than anyone. As Mum swept over to him and ushered him back into their room to unpack, she was still telling him how wonderfully the hamster we'd just seen dash off to eat one of the hotel's expensive floral displays was doing back at home.

Once the bedroom door closed, Dad crouched down beside us, apparently not thinking to ask what we were doing lying on the floor with a shoebox, a shopping bag and a pair of my brother's pants. 'Don't let him hear about it, but the hamster's gone missing,' Dad hissed. 'Gran's just called in a flap.'

Oh. *Oh.*

I sat up. 'We *know* the hamster's missing, Dad. We—'

'Got a call too, did you?' he interrupted. 'Well, never mind – she's calmed down now. I've got her emailing pet shops with a photo, looking for one he'd pick out of an identity parade.'

'No, Dad – the hamster just—'

I fell silent in the face of my dad putting his finger to his lips and blowing a long, loud *SHHHHHHHHH* at me.

Well. I supposed if nothing else, this meant Grandma would be buying the fake Fluffy, not Kayla and me. Hopefully Mum would be in there bamboozling Jude into believing he'd never smuggled the hamster out to begin with.

Dad started to get up, holding out a hand to Kayla, who'd managed to get a leg stuck in the bag I'd been using for a makeshift hamster net. Once he'd straightened her up, he picked up his bags and headed into the bedroom, looking back to add, 'Oh, and there was a load of fuss in the hallway when we came back. Some fight about keeping a drum kit in the bathroom. Looks like your Nightmares are a couple of rooms down the hall.'

Kayla fell straight back over again.

From the look on her face, Dad had no idea how right he was.

EIGHT

'It's not that I don't want to be near the band. In fact, being near them is *exactly* what I want,' Kayla was saying, as we climbed out of the car and waved Jude and my parents off the next morning, after a long night of not being allowed to order room service because they were both *totally* stingy and unfair. 'It's just the pressure of having to be prepared to impress them at all times. I like to know precisely when I need to be ready to dazzle. I like a regime. That's why Summer and I didn't work.'

Summer was a girl Kayla had dated for a bit recently. They'd got together on the last night at Starcross Sands, the same holiday park where I'd met Leo. Summer had liked flower crowns and yoga, and had liked Kayla more than Kayla had been able to like her back.

'Because she didn't understand the spreadsheet you made, *Tabulating Potential Date Locations by Proximity, Financial Viability and Romantic Possibility*?' I asked.

'Partly.' Kayla nodded. 'She was nice but a tiny bit *too* free-spirited. I like spirits with a healthy appreciation of rules and rational order.'

'Sounds romantic. Remind me how you're a death-metal fan, again?'

Deathsplash weren't exactly the most orderly band in the world. There was a rumour that Rick Deathsplash once destroyed so many instruments onstage that the band had to play the rest of the set using their own YouTube videos as a backing track.

'It's *organized* chaos,' Kayla said, as she followed me into the training centre Feet of the Future were using for the week. 'That's my favourite kind. It just *looks* out of control while, in reality, every single explosion and smashed guitar is carefully planned. There's quite an art to it.'

I raised my eyebrows. 'Well, maybe you can tell them how much you admire their organizational skills if we bump into them at the hotel. Ask them if they need any spreadsheets made.'

'Very funny,' Kayla said, rolling her eyes. 'Anyway, it's highly unlikely to happen. They're probably not allowed to get out of the shower without a fleet of bodyguards, let alone run into randoms in the corridors.'

The training centre wasn't as impressive as Old Trafford, but it was still pretty huge. Easily as big as my school, but totally devoted to football. Feet of the Future was being held indoors somewhere, on an artificial pitch with its own terraces and everything. I'd never played on an indoor pitch before. I had to admit I was interested to see what it was like.

Kayla stopped in front of two sets of paper arrows that had been clipped to a pinboard on the wall, one labelled *FOTF* and one *CC*. They each pointed in opposite directions. 'Well, here's where we split up.'

'I still can't believe you're going to Camp Cheer!' I told her.

She smiled sweetly at me. 'Of course you can't. Because I'm not.'

'Not what?'

Kayla sighed, as if I'd somehow missed something I should have known all along. 'Dylan, I'm *obviously* not going to the cheerleading classes. I hate enforced perk. And frankly I think it's insulting that the boys all do sport, and the girls are expected to jump around making pyramids and wearing flippy skirts.'

This was starting to get really confusing. 'But there are boys in Camp Cheer too – though I don't think they wear flippy skirts. Cheerleading is a sport. And there's a girls' football camp you could have gone to, if you'd wanted.'

'But I don't like football.' Kayla was speaking to me slowly, the way she does when she teaches Jude big words.

'You don't like cheerleading either.'

'Exactly – and that's why I'm doing neither. I'm going to find an empty room and start working on my props for the Ghoulish Games competition. I'm going to have to make this a full-time job if I'm going to win. And I *am* going to win. Rick Deathsplash is as good as sweating on me already.'

I tried not to pull a face at that. The plan still didn't quite add up. 'You need props? But what are you going to make? We didn't bring anything with us.'

'I brought *three suitcases*,' she snapped. 'What did you *think* I had in them? Three different sets of pom-poms?'

I hadn't really thought about it, if I was honest. I'd just assumed that number of cases was normal for girls. 'I don't know – make-up?'

Kayla tutted. 'I know I used to wear a lot, Dylan, but not *actually* an industrial amount. Now that I've stopped using all that concealer to cover my birthmark, I've cut down to just the one suitcase full. I call it, *embracing my natural beauty.*'

I rolled my eyes at the sarcasm, but Kayla was still in full flow.

'Anyway, I'd better go before someone notices I'm out of place and tries to draft me into something horrific involving mud and flat footwear.' Unzipping the huge kitbag she'd slung over her shoulder, she pulled out a printed sign that read *DO NOT ENTER: SPORTS IN PROGRESS* and waved it proudly at me. 'This should be all I need to secure an empty room. I'll come and find you at the end of the day.'

'But—' I said, as she headed back along the hall.

'See you later!' she trilled happily, the door sliding closed in her wake.

I stared at the door for a long time, choking down a knot of worry that she'd get in trouble, before finally slumping round to follow the arrows towards Feet of the Future.

Before I could get much further, I heard the door opening again, and turned without even trying to hide my relief that Kayla hadn't actually gone off on her own. 'I *knew* you wouldn't leave me . . .' I started.

And then stopped, struck silent by the curious smile on Freddie Alton's face.

'*Never*,' he said, clutching a hand to his heart. 'Your dad's as extra as my mum is. I need you around to make me look good.'

I just stood there, my mouth making curious twisted shapes around words that weren't managing to happen. He was *talking to me*, and not even just to laugh at the weirdly romantic greeting I'd accidentally given him. At least, my brain–mouth coordination *had been* working, before I knew *who* I was talking to.

After a moment, he frowned at my clammy silence. 'Sorry – you must get people taking the piss out of you over it all the time. I know I do. You *are* from school, right? Dylan Kershaw. I remember I was going to scout you for the first team before that incident that got you banned from extra-curricular sport.'

I inwardly grimaced. That *incident* had involved Dad protesting a referee's bad decision by pelting him with an egg sandwich, thankfully gone soft and soggy from having spent the whole match in Dad's pocket. The only damage done was to the ref's shirt and my school football career. I couldn't believe Freddie Alton *knew*.

More than that, he *knew who I was*.

It was terrifying. Up till now, I'd been perfectly happy existing in mute obscurity, never having to fear clamming up under the pressure of a tricky question like *How are you?* or *All right, Dylan?*

I had to *do* something; I couldn't just stand there woodenly – part boy, part plank.

So I coughed.

Freddie carried on. 'It was a shame – you were really good.'

Then he stopped, as I went on coughing.

And coughing.

'. . . Are you all right?' he asked, finally.

Weakly, I pointed to my throat and made a helpless

croaking sound. Funnily enough, it actually was quite sore now. Fake coughing for five minutes can be pretty rough.

'Oh – sore throat?' Freddie asked.

I nodded.

'You're not contagious, are you?'

I shook my head.

'Oh,' Freddie said. 'Pity.'

And he started off down the hall before I could even try to find the words to ask what he meant.

Following him, we walked out on to the fake turf of the indoor pitch, where a load of other boys were already lining up to be registered. Freddie jogged towards the group.

And I froze, realizing he wasn't the *only* person here I'd met before.

NINE

A boy not much older than me with flame-red hair and an upturned nose that made his face look about ten years younger than the rest of him was taking the register. He stood ticking off names from a list, one by one, until an older man stalked across the pitch and grabbed the papers from his hand.

I knew who *he* was, obviously. I'd seen him plenty of times on *Match of the Day*, and once or twice when Mum was watching the evening news. His name was Jez Dutton, and he used to be a top-flight player . . . until he drove through the front of his neighbour's house and ran over their dog one night while apparently trying to back into his own drive.

According to the stories on the front of all the papers, he'd been on his way back from an all-you-can-eat curry night at the local pub and had been urgently trying to get home to the loo when he misjudged where his driveway was. He'd backed up straight through next door's net curtains. He couldn't see where he was going properly through the spice sweats.

He got away with a big fine, and he paid for the

neighbour's dog to have wheels fitted on both back legs, but it didn't stop the papers running headlines like 'LUNATIKKA' and 'VINDALOONEY'. The club fired him, and he hadn't been picked up anywhere else. It looked like he'd given up to become an academy teacher now.

I had to admit, it was going to be pretty cool to be taught by an actual celebrity, even if he was mostly famous for accident-by-overeating. The pub had said Jez's capacity for putting away curries was 'practically superhuman'.

But Jez Dutton hadn't been the person I'd recognized first.

'Come on, sunshine – if your legs don't work, we'll have to send you home!' he yelled across the pitch at me.

Realizing I hadn't moved since I'd first walked in, I slung my bag back across my shoulder and ran to join everyone else in the line, shooting anxious glances down the row to see if I'd been noticed too.

'Eyes front!' Jez snapped, stalking back and forth in front of us. 'When I'm talking, I'm the only person who exists in your world. I'm your coach, and that means while you're here, I'm your god. Got it? So don't let me catch your attention wandering. Now, I'm going to call out some names, and when you hear yours, you'll call back, "Yes, Jez." Understand?'

'Yes, Jez,' most of us chorused.

He sniffed and turned his head to spit on the pitch before nodding and continuing. 'Good. Now then – let's find out who wasn't man enough to show up once they found out I'*d* be the one whipping you into shape. Aaron Addington.'

'Yes, Jez,' a voice called from the other end of the line. Aaron was tall and pale, with spiky black hair and an expression as eager as a Labrador waiting for someone to throw a ball.

'Freddie Alton.'

'Yes, Jez,' Freddie called, somehow sounding cool and casual enough that he could have been talking to one of his mates. I couldn't quite help the thrill I got every time I remembered we were actually going to be on a team together, even though feeling thrilled somehow made me feel a bit guilty too.

Jez went on down the list, calling out names faster and faster, until the replies started tipping into each other, like dominoes. 'Chidi Daku, Laurie Deering –' Laurie was the boy who'd been taking the register – 'Josh Egham, Azi Fayose . . .'

'YesJezYesJezYesJezYesJezYesJez.'

Then Jez stopped. He cleared his throat and squinted at the registration list before reading out very, very slowly, 'Fauntleroy Genghis Charlemagne Hughes.'

All along the line, people shifted and turned to peer at what turned out not to be four boys, but just one.

One I knew.

Fauntleroy Genghis Charlemagne Hughes blushed and pushed a hand back through his messy blond hair. 'Um, it's just Leroy, actually. Mum got a bit obsessed with ancestry.com and named me after everyone we might be related to – um – I mean . . . Yes, Jez?'

'Yes, Jez,' Jez growled, ripping off the sheet of paper with the first set of names on it and handing it to Laurie. 'Get that nonsense corrected to something I can pronounce.'

As the boy got busy with a biro, Jez continued with the register, but I wasn't listening any more. I'd been hoping that I'd made some kind of mistake, that there were lots of slightly anxious-seeming boys with haircuts that looked like they'd have been fashionable a couple of centuries ago, and I'd just got a couple of them mixed up. But those hopes had vanished as soon as Jez had squinted at that name.

I wasn't going to forget the only Fauntleroy I'd ever met – *especially* one who'd been friends with the boy I'd had a planet-sized crush on last summer.

And I didn't mean Leo. There had been someone else, first.

Someone who'd made me think I might have had

a chance with him . . . before he called me a 'gaylord' in front of a whole swimming pool full of people and assorted inflatable animals. He'd insulted Kayla, too. And his little brother had been something small and malevolent you shouldn't feed after midnight.

Jayden-Lee Slater.

I'd thought he was my dream boy for a while, but he turned out to be a waking nightmare. Even if he'd made up for it a tiny bit before we left. Leroy had been one of the gang he'd hung out with. And that meant he'd been at the pool when Jayden-Lee had fallen about laughing over me being gay, like it was the big punchline of the sitcom episode that was my life.

I was pretty sure that meant Leroy had been laughing too.

And even if I was sort of over that – and didn't wake up in the middle of the night with flashbacks of ornamental flamingos and inflatable bananas burned on to the backs of my eyelids very often any more – it meant something more important *now*.

After sort of coming out over the summer – to my parents, anyway – I was being a bit more open about being gay. I didn't see why I had to be scared or ashamed of something just because other people might think I should be. So all my friends at school knew now, and quite a few people who weren't really my friends but liked to have the latest gossip. It had all been a lot easier than I'd expected. There wasn't much fuss. They hadn't run a headline in the school paper: 'BREAKING NEWS: DYLAN KISSED A BOY, AND HE LIKED IT'.

So far, it had turned out that not that many people thought it was a huge deal, and that was exactly how I wanted it to be. But I liked to be able to choose when I told people too. And football was still somewhere I hadn't quite figured out how to be *all* of me: the part that kicked awesome penalties and the part that kissed awesome boys just never seemed to mix. Football was somewhere I still couldn't be sure what people would think.

And anyway, it's not like I was just going to walk in and announce it. *Hi, I'm Dylan Kershaw. I'm nearly fifteen, and if I had to play Kiss, Marry or Kill with the Avengers, all three of my answers would start with Chris.*

But now it looked like I wouldn't get the choice of keeping it quiet, either.

I could feel my good mood deflating. There was even a hissing sound as it went down, like a sad balloon the day after a party. *Pssssst.*

'Psssst.' Or maybe that was Freddie Alton, hissing down the line at me.

Startled, I snapped out of my worries to hear, 'Kershaw . . . Has Dylan Kershaw not turned up? Right.

59

First pathetic wuss of the day: Dylan Kershaw.'

And I watched him underline my name.

'I'm not a pathetic wuss. I mean, I'm here. I mean – yes, Jez?' I yelped.

Jez looked up to scowl at me, his forehead folding into a series of leathery wrinkles. 'Bit late for that. Better not put you in goal – you'll stick your hand out for the ball ten minutes after the other team have finished celebrating.'

A low chuckle went down the line. I could feel my ears heating up.

'Sorry. I'm not actually a goalie, anyway, so . . . I wasn't listening – that's all.'

And that was definitely, totally the wrong excuse to use. Jez raised his eyebrows, concertinaing his forehead wrinkles even more.

'What did you just say?'

Ten minutes later, I was running laps round the edge of the pitch while the others chatted about what numbers and positions they wanted for the big match at the end of the week.

Somehow, I didn't think I was off to a very good start.

TEN

The whole morning was set aside for warm-up exercises, even though I'd got so warm during my punishment laps that it felt like I might be starting to melt. I lost count of how many Jez made me run before he let me join everyone else, but after a while, I'd begun to sympathize with the way Jude's hamster must feel when he gets stuck on his wheel.

After that, we'd lined up to do a set of drills where we had to dodge colourful cones and dribble a practice ball around yet another circuit, while Jez stood on the sidelines eating a bacon sandwich and yelling, 'FASTER. PICK UP THE PACE, YOU BARREL OF NUMPTIES!' at us every five minutes.

I asked Chidi and Josh: none of us knew what a numpty even was.

After each circuit, we had to run up the pitch and kick the ball through the open goal. Even without a defender, I was the only one to get every shot home. The circuit had been designed to make us too tired and dizzy to focus properly, but striking was my speciality. I even tried out a few confusion tactics I'd use if there *had* been a goalie – making it look like I was aiming for one side of the net, then slamming the ball into the other.

I checked Jez's expression each time I scored, hoping to make up a bit for having messed up over the register. It was weird, though. The more shots I got on target, the less pleased he looked.

Finally, when we were all so red and out of breath that we looked like a bunch of deflating balloons in spiked boots, a murmur started to go round the other boys. Some of them were nudging each other and looking like they were trying not to laugh, while others just stared off to one side of the pitch.

I jogged up to see what the fuss was about. From the dark of the players entrance, a figure was emerging. A slight – and slightly orange – figure, with highlighter-yellow hair and a short dress made from what looked like the feathers of a flock of pink ducklings.

A very, *very* short dress.

Lacey Laine, Jez Dutton's long-term girlfriend, hadn't dumped him when the Premier League did. In fact, even though he wasn't officially a player any more, she was still in the news all the time as one of a glamorous group of footballers' wives and girlfriends. They'd even had their own TV show for a while: *WAG Tales*.

I didn't totally get the whole 'wives and girlfriends' thing. Or, actually, what I didn't get was why boyfriends and husbands never made the same effort. It looked like WAGS had an amazing time, but you never saw groups of players' boyfriends out shopping in Selfridges, wearing flimsy outfits to show off their back waxes, and piling into exclusive restaurants for fancy lunches.

If Leo ever became an ultra-famous dancer, I was *definitely* going to invent a new celebrity acronym just for us. It would have to be one that worked for either gender, too. Like POD – Partner of Dancer. I'd be a brilliant POD. I could give gossipy magazine interviews and have my photo taken laughing with salads all day.

That is, if we were still together then. I wasn't even really sure whether I was a POD *now*.

Trying to keep the gloom from setting in, I stood next to Chidi and watched as Lacey Laine skipped over to Jez. She gave him a pink-lipsticked kiss on the cheek, deposited what looked like a paper-bag lunch from some sort of artisan deli in his arms (it had a bunch of celery sticking out of one corner, like weirdly unromantic flowers), and sat down on the subs bench behind him with a copy of *MOXY magazine*.

'I don't know what you lot are looking at!' Jez yelled, knowing exactly what all of us were looking at – though I might have been the only one of us wondering how someone got their skin that shade of orange. Maybe she bathed in the blood of baby carrots.

'Lunch, *now*!' Jez shouted.

So we broke to get lunch. Just like at school, Freddie was instantly the centre of a crowd of the tallest, fittest, fastest boys, all of them jostling with each other to make the loudest joke or get the spot by his side. Popularity is so weird. It's like some people are just born with a golden glow, and everyone else can't help but want to hang around them, hoping it might rub off.

If I glowed at all, it was just the remaining sheen of sweat caused by those laps.

I hung back while Chidi announced to everyone in the changing room that he'd heard there would be football scouts from professional teams coming to the match at the end of the week, and Laurie said he'd be happy playing any position as long as it was centre forward. Then, once they'd all grabbed their lunches and headed back to sit in the stands, I went to pick up mine. This way, everyone would already have picked their spot, and I could choose my own carefully. I needed to be somewhere far enough away from Freddie that I wouldn't have to talk to him, *and* far enough away that Leroy wouldn't try to talk to me.

'Hello! I've been meaning to talk to you all morning,' Leroy chirped, wandering out of the shower block to my right. 'Are we the only ones still here?'

I let my head drop into my hands and sat down on

one of the benches. So much for plans.

Leroy sat next to me, sliding out a small wicker basket and starting to rifle through it. It looked like an old-fashioned picnic hamper. 'Have you got a headache? Hold on, I should have something for that in here.'

'No, I'm fine,' I murmured, distracted. 'Is that where you keep your kit?'

Leroy emerged triumphant with three packets of pills in his hand – headaches, sore throats and constipation all seemed to be covered. 'No. I keep my kit in my *kitbag*, silly. This is where I keep my picnics.'

One of the sides of his basket was still flipped back. I looked down to see a selection of sandwiches, what looked like mini sausage rolls and scotch eggs, and a tub of chocolate fingers, all laid out in Tupperware.

'Mum says I get very tetchy if I don't have a decent lunch,' he explained. 'No headache? How about some crisps?'

I only had a boiled egg and a bread roll scavenged from the breakfast buffet in my bag, but I couldn't stick around. Any minute now, he'd remember his question.

'I'm OK, thank y— Are those roast beef?'

'King of the Monster Munches,' Leroy agreed, offering the bag. 'Anyway, I was wondering if you were still dating that dancing hamster?'

I'd started reaching for a crisp before the bottom

plummeted out of my stomach, and now I was stuck with one hand in mid-air, no longer hungry but not wanting to look like I was dissing his picnic. I took a crisp and let it crumble in my fingers before I managed to find an answer.

'Um, sort of. He's not *actually* a hamster.'

'He was most of the times I met him,' Leroy pointed out, digging out an egg sandwich and tucking in as though this was a totally normal conversation to have. 'How do you *sort-of* date someone? I saw you kissing at that dance.'

I didn't want my memories of that kiss with Leo tangled up with whatever Leroy was going to say about it. I didn't want him to laugh at something that still definitely counted as one of the best nights of my life, whatever might happen between me and Leo in the future.

But I didn't want to pretend it was nothing either, just to throw Leroy off the scent. It would be even worse if I messed up my memories for myself. It wasn't nothing. It was . . .

It was *everything*.

'We're supposed to be seeing each other,' I admitted, finally. 'We just haven't had much of a chance to actually *see* each other since the summer. He's really busy.'

I shifted uncomfortably on the bench and swallowed

the remains of the Monster Munch, hoping it might clear whatever felt like it was stuck in my throat. 'I – um – don't talk about it much . . .'

'Oh, that's OK,' Leroy said brightly. 'I understand. I just thought it was kind of cool.'

'Cool?' I asked, not quite sure if this was the build-up to a joke at my expense.

'Well, yeah. You kissing like that in front of everyone. Like – I've got two aunts, and only one of them's related to me. Do you know what I mean?'

I guessed he probably didn't mean one aunt was married to an uncle. Still, this conversation wasn't going anywhere I'd expected, and I wasn't certain I hadn't got lost somewhere along the way. So I said, 'I think so. They're gay?'

'Right! So it's cool you're cool about it.' Leroy smiled. 'Some people get really weird about that kind of thing. Anyway, I'm going to see if anyone wants one of my cocktail sausages. Want to come?'

He almost skipped out on to the stands.

And, after a minute of blinking at a row of jockstraps, not *quite* sure what had just happened, I got up to follow him.

Just as Jez Dutton appeared, red-faced, in the doorway.

ELEVEN

I got another fifteen laps for 'not being a team player' and 'failing to participate in bonding exercises' because Jez thought I'd been hiding so I could eat lunch alone. Jez wouldn't tolerate shyness, he'd shouted, loudly enough to make every single person in the stands stare at me.

By the time we were let out that afternoon, we'd played fifteen minutes of football and I'd ploughed a Dylan-sized groove around the edges of the pitch. Kayla was waiting for me by the park-and-ride bus stop outside. It stopped right by our hotel, so my parents were fine with us getting it back together. She was carrying the same oversized kitbag, but I thought it seemed more suspiciously bulky than it had that morning. She was looking totally innocent, though, as we got on and found a seat by the window.

Just as the bus began to pull away, everyone who'd *really* gone to Camp Cheer began spilling out through the academy doors. They were laughing and chatting – it seemed like the cheer coach might have been a little bit nicer than Jez.

I nudged Kayla. 'You weren't wrong – some of them *are* wearing flippy skirts.'

Although a lot of the girls were just wearing tracksuits, and there were a couple of boys in the group who didn't seem to have opted for anything pleated and thigh-high either.

Kayla hummed non-committally. 'It's not the outfits, Dylan; it's the principle. Can't you see how happy they look?'

I leaned over to peer judgementally though the window. 'Ah, I see. So it's the *cheer* part you object to.'

'Only enforced cheer,' Kayla corrected. 'I object to smiling just because twenty people with glossy hair and overly white teeth recite a rhyming couplet telling me I should. If I'm not happy, it's only going to irritate me. And if I am, it might make my genuine smile seem fake. It's a lose-lose situation, Dylan.'

'I just thought you might want to go and make some friends,' I said, shrugging.

Kayla paused. 'I have more important things to do. Even if they do look nice.'

'I thought you said they had overly white teeth?'

'I mean they look like nice *people*.' She tutted. 'Nice isn't a physical characteristic. Although . . .' She was leaning out of her seat now, turning to get a last glimpse of a few cheerleaders shaking their pom-poms in the air.

'I suppose the other sense applies too.'

'Oh, no.' I shook my head. 'I've changed my mind. Forget Camp Cheer. It'll be like when you played the flute for six weeks, dated half the school orchestra, and caused that incident in assembly where Sam Brolin clapped Ameet Gupta's ears between his cymbals. Besides, what if you ended up in a long-distance relationship with someone from *Manchester*! Long-distance relationships are hard, you know. That time our internet went down for the weekend, I nearly pined away with missing Leo.'

It was true. I hadn't been able to eat dessert when we went out for Sunday lunch, and Mum insisted on taking my temperature when we got home. I was fine, though. Just lovesick.

'Well, I wouldn't mind *some* sort of relationship,' Kayla said, sounding wistful. 'I've been living in total social isolation since ending things with Summer. Like those gurus who meditate on rocks for months at a time.'

I didn't know a lot of gurus, but I hadn't heard of a meditation technique devoted to playing death metal at decibel levels loud enough to deafen the neighbours, or dealing with bad days by downing 'crispy cocktails' – stacks of Pringles loaded with sour Haribo (Kayla said it was going to be the new salted caramel of the food-trend world). Still, I didn't try to argue.

'Nice to know being friends with me counts as "total social isolation". What about using an app or something, if there's no one you like at school?'

She looked at me out of the corner of her eye. 'First of all, I'm almost certain that's not legal when you're fifteen, and I don't want to ruin my bright future as a top barrister because I wanted to swipe a few strangers. And second, don't they make you write a cheesy tag line about yourself on those? What would I say?'

'How about, "Kayla: always fresh, always tasty"?'

'Did you just read that off the window of the bakery over there?'

'No?' I averted my eyes from the line-up of sausage rolls and steak slices and turned my attention to the shops on the other side of the street.

Kayla folded her arms. 'OK, so what other suggestions do you have for me?'

I groped frantically for an idea. It was no good: I had to scan the shop fronts for help. 'Ummm. "Kayla: pick one up for pennies"?'

She shoved me and shook her head. 'I think we're done here. Except – Dylan, what were they selling in that takeaway?'

I craned my neck to look back at the street we'd just passed. 'I don't know which one you mean. Why?'

'Were they selling chicken? I'm *sure* they were selling chicken.'

'They might have been.' I shrugged. 'Why does it matter?'

Ignoring my question, Kayla was already standing and pressing her thumb firmly to the button on the bar in front of us. '*Stop the bus – we have to get off!*'

It's incredible how things can go from normal to crazy in the space of a second. Kayla's cry must have sounded urgent enough that the bus driver thought there was some kind of emergency. He slammed on the brakes and a busload of people were thrown backwards.

A woman in a puffa jacket that took up two seats all by itself started to panic. 'Is it a fire? There's a fire! Fire!'

Then a busload of people threw themselves forward, tumbling and climbing over each other in an effort to evacuate as the bus doors slid open.

Kayla and I were the last to get off. Which made sense, since we were the only ones who knew nothing was burning. The bus driver came charging up the aisle towards us, his eyes wild.

'What is it? What's happened?!'

'Oh, nothing, really,' Kayla said, and she pointed out of the window. 'I just didn't want to get too far away from the chicken shop.'

For someone who'd just found out that his bus

wasn't about to burn down, the driver didn't seem too delighted. He pointed at the doors in silence.

Minutes later, we were standing outside Chick'n Mansion, with a busload of freshly reseated people staring angrily out at us from behind brightly lit windows.

I wasn't sure about eating food from a place that didn't even use the real word for 'chicken' in its name. It sounded like it might be a way to avoid breaking the Trade Descriptions Act. But the adrenaline from our public transport adventure took my mind off any potential food poisoning to come.

'That was like an action film,' I said. 'I think there's one where they're stuck on a bus. I don't remember anybody getting a lecture about abusing public services from someone's grandad in that one, though.'

'I stand by my actions,' Kayla said loftily. 'It's not my fault the driver overreacted. Nobody was hurt, and we only had a two-minute stroll to pick up a Chick'n Banquet.'

'You know, we're probably going to have dinner back at the hotel . . .' I started.

'We're not getting dinner!' Kayla said, as if food was the last reason anyone would go to a takeaway. 'This is for the Deathsplash Nightmares!'

I looked up at the window menu of cheap chick'n

delights. 'Aren't they rich enough to get their own meals?'

'The contest, Dylan. I meant this is for the contest. The first challenge is to take a haunted photo.'

'And you just happened to see something in the window of the chicken shop? If it's some long-dead rooster come back for revenge, I might have to think about going vegetarian again.'

'Not quite.' Kayla was grinning. She whipped a white sheet with black eyeholes cut out of it from her kitbag and passed it to me. 'You're going to be the ghost. I have to stand out from the crowd somehow, Dylan, and however many people I'm up against, I think I can guarantee no one else will be entering a poultrygeist!'

TWELVE

Chick'n Mansion was heaving. It felt like everyone in Manchester had decided on smok'y wingz for dinner. The sound system was playing ancient 80s pop, and the stools at the window were fully occupied by people stuffing their faces. Kayla went in ahead of me, since the plan was that she'd take up a position near the counter and snap pictures while I placed an order, making sure to get everyone's reactions to seeing a ghost.

Personally, I was pretty sure the main reaction would be laughter. I looked more like someone who'd been assaulted by the contents of a washing line than anything vaguely scary. I touched my face, grateful for the sheet covering it, took a deep breath to settle my nerves, and pushed my way inside.

At first, no one seemed to notice a spook in a stolen bedsheet joining the queue for food. Maybe it just wasn't the most unusual sight in Manchester that night. It was nearly Halloween, after all – the city might have gone mad for costume parties.

Then a couple of people joined the line behind me, and I heard someone loudly clear their throat. I looked round to see a boy in a shirt and tie, a couple of years younger than me, and a couple of feet shorter. He looked like he was such a fan of his school uniform that he'd forgotten to take it off. Standing next to him was a friendly looking older lady, who was knitting as she queued.

'Bit disrespectful, isn't it?' the boy said.

I wouldn't have known what to reply even if I hadn't had a bedsheet over my mouth. I stared blankly at him through my big black eyeholes.

'I said, it's a bit *disrespectful*,' he repeated, louder. 'That costume.'

Then he leaned in, gesturing to the whole ensemble with a sweep of his hands. 'I mean, a ghost.' He paused. 'My nan's very old.'

I slid my eyes slowly across to his nan, who was probably about sixty. She smiled, not exactly looking like she was about to don a sheet of her own and head off haunting any time soon.

Not knowing what else to do, I smiled and said, 'Sorry?' then turned back around to find the crowds in front of me had all been served, and I was now at the front.

'Can I take your order . . . sir?' The girl behind the counter had started speaking before she'd noticed what I was wearing.

I pointed helplessly at the menu, indicating the Bitz N Bitez Banquet, while she covered her mouth with her hand and tried to pretend she wasn't laughing.

This was so embarrassing. Kayla could dress up in her own stupid costumes next time. I looked over to where she was waiting by the wall and caught the flash of a photo being taken.

Unfortunately I also caught the eye of suit-and-tie boy, who'd moved to the counter next to me. He cleared his throat noisily again, and I quickly stared the other way. I just had to avoid looking at him until I got my food, then I was vanishing out of here. If I could have spirited myself away into the ether, I would have.

It would be a really useful skill to have, vanishing. If I could just disappear from the corporeal plane whenever Freddie Alton said a polite hello, or Jez Dutton fixed me with a random and totally unprovoked death glare, it would make my life *so* much easier.

Unfortunately, there was no chance of vanishing now. I was a bit too conspicuous for that.

'Are you looking at me?' someone snapped.

I dragged myself out of my supernatural superpower daydreams to focus on her.

'You *are*!' She pointed and nudged her mates. 'He is! Hey, look. Casper the overfriendly ghost over there's been staring at me for ages.'

'Are you looking at my mate?' A girl in black lace-up leggings and a dress that looked like she'd sprayed it on before leaving the house stepped forward.

'What are you looking at? Do I look funny to you?' the first girl asked, flicking her bouncy blond curls in fury.

'He was looking at my nan too!' chimed in the boy from behind me.

That was the last straw.

'*Why* would I be looking at your nan?' I snapped, loud enough to be heard through the cloth.

'So now there's something wrong with my nan?' the boy demanded.

I threw up my hands. Nobody was making any sense. 'I just wasn't looking at her!' Snatching up the tub of chicken on the counter, I turned to try to make my escape. 'I don't want to look at any of you, I swear!'

The girl in the skintight dress made a choking noise. 'So you're calling me ugly now?'

'Are you being offensive to Shannon?' Another girl with a high ponytail swishing at the back of her head entered the fray, marching right up to me. 'That's rich, coming from you in your stupid dress.'

'It's not a dress –' I started, trying to look for a way out, or to catch Kayla's eye and get her to help me somehow.

She was nowhere to be seen.

'It's not a suit and tie, is it?' Shannon sneered.

I could practically feel the boy beside me radiating smugness.

The third girl smacked the bottom of my takeaway tub. Twelve pieces of chicken in bright red hot sauce leaped up and hit me in the chest.

'Right, I've told you kids, I'm not having messing about in my shop.' The owner swung up the counter and stormed through. He must have been about six foot, and as broad-chested as he was tall. He looked like a brick wall in an apron. 'Who started this?'

'He was staring at me.'

'He said I was ugly!'

'He dissed my nan.'

'It's not even a proper dress.'

The chorus of complaints went off at once, and the owner fixed his eyes on me. I tried to run for it, dodging round Shannon and getting ready to hurdle over the top of suit-and-tie, when two massive hands gripped the back of my sheet – and the shirt under it – lifting me off the floor.

As I skidded to a stop, face first on the pavement outside with chick'n pieces scattered around me like sticky-coated shrapnel, Kayla bounded over and took a final photo.

'That was *brilliant*, Dylan!' She beamed. 'I *knew* you'd make a great ghost, but I didn't expect you to find a way to *fly*!'

THIRTEEN

By the time Kayla had finished using the ghostly sheet to wipe hot sauce out of my hair, and we'd caught another bus, we were an hour late getting back to the hotel. I wasn't sure if my stomach was churning with worry over how livid my parents were going to be, or because of the leftover chick'n pieces I'd eaten on the way.

I needn't have worried, though. Mum and Dad got back later than we did. The door to the suite flew open just as I was tapping out a **Where are you?** text.

They had Jude with them, leading the way. I'd expected him to look a bit tired after his day with Whizzy Wheels, but he looked white as paper. This was in contrast to Mum, behind him, who was flushed with delight.

'What kept you?' I asked, letting my tone imply we'd been waiting ages without actually having to lie.

'*Spooky Doings!*' Mum replied, clasping her hands together.

'Isn't that a TV show?' Kayla interjected. 'You could have watched it up here.'

It was Mum's *favourite* TV show. A sort of documentary where nothing ever happened. Every week, the team would show up in a new location – usually an ancient Tudor manor or a derelict church, and spend a few nights sitting in the dark being scared of nothing in particular. I was nearly sure they'd never caught a ghost on camera, but there were always enough mysterious tapping noises and chairs that might have moved a tiny bit to keep Mum hooked.

In my opinion, *Spooky Doings* spent more time proving ghosts didn't exist than they did, but that didn't seem to matter to Mum. She was beaming.

'Not the TV Show – *real* spooky doings! Can you believe it? The hotel is haunted!'

'Your mother's been reading to us from their pamphlets,' Dad put in, sounding like this was some form of torture. 'Apparently, there's a famous ghost.'

'Here? Really?' I frowned. 'Don't ghosts usually go in for places with oak beams and ancient graveyards, rather than en suite showers and a breakfast buffet?'

'Apparently this hotel was built on the foundations of somewhere much older,' Mum said, dropping her voice. 'A Tudor lodge that burned down in mysterious circumstances. They say that even now guests often complain of smelling smoke near the kitchens, or spot Mary the maid in a dress lit up by flames . . .'

'The restaurant has a barbecue menu, doesn't it?' Kayla asked.

'It might,' Mum said, slightly sharply. 'Though I don't see what that has to do with anything. Anyway, don't you think it's exciting? I might go ghost hunting tomorrow night!'

'Speaking of barbecue –' I cut in, because I'd definitely rather talk about that than how quickly Mum could get us thrown out of the hotel by stalking spectres through the halls – 'weren't we supposed to be going out to eat about now?'

At the word *eat*, Jude let out a soft whimper. I looked at him for a moment, then carried on cautiously.

'Only . . . I said I'd speak to Leo at eight, and I don't want to miss him.'

'Right, yeah. About dinner . . .' Dad said.

Jude whimpered again, louder this time.

'About . . . *that*,' Dad tried, looking worried. 'We've decided the plans we had weren't exactly ideal.'

'What? Why?' I'd been looking forward to eating downstairs, or at least to eating something nice enough to take the terrible chick'ny taste out of my mouth. 'Are there bad reviews for the restaurant or something?'

I barely finished my sentence. At the word *restaurant*, Jude wailed loudly and swooned to one side, pressing his pale face against the side of his chair.

Mum crouched down and smoothed her hands through his hair: a tried-and-tested comfort technique she'd used since he was a baby. 'Well, exciting as the hotel having its own personal haunting is, it's made Jude a little anxious about the restaurant.'

That explained things. Jude was pretty easily freaked out. He believed there was a monster under his bed for so long that we gave it a name and made up a boring day job for it as an accountant. Eventually we told him it decided to move away for a shorter commute, and it hadn't bothered him since.

'What would a ghoul be doing in a kitchen, anyway?' I asked, as Mum and Dad shot me *please don't make this worse* looks. 'Making *spook*ghetti?'

Jude glanced up from his woeful slump.

Kayla glared at me. I could tell she was just jealous I'd outdone her *poultrygeist* pun.

'Don't be daft,' she said. 'It must be stealing all the *boo*-berry pies.'

I had to admit that was well played, even if it was seriously annoying. How did she just come up with these? I'd nearly done a victory dance when I'd thought of spookghetti.

The most important thing, though, was that Jude had almost forgotten his fears and cracked a smile.

'Even so, we thought we'd stay in with room service

tonight,' Dad said, unaware that he was making another of my dream holiday wishes come true. Room service! And all it had taken was making a five-year-old too scared to leave the suite.

'We'll try the restaurant again in the morning,' he said. 'For some bacon and . . . *egg-toplasm.*'

Jude, Kayla and I wrinkled our noses at the exact same time.

'Doesn't really work, Dad,' I said.

Kayla nodded. 'Just sounds a bit gross.'

And we went to grab the room-service menu, leaving Dad to google 'best dad jokes of all time' so he'd be prepared for the next pun-off.

Once we'd ordered, I shut the door to my room and texted Leo to see if he'd be around earlier than we'd agreed.

Hey, are you there?

I waited a couple of minutes. He was probably still stuck in rehearsals. The last few nights, they'd been running really late, and I'd been trying to feel sorry for him about that. *Poor* Leo, having *no* fun. Being *forced* to dance all day with no holiday at *all.*

It could be a little bit difficult to work up much

sympathy when he kept telling me how much he loved doing it, and what a 'cool group' the people he was working with were, but I was sure that was just him making it sound better than it was, so as not to worry me. Leo didn't even *like* cool people, anyway. He liked *me*.

(I really hoped he still liked me.)

Finally, my phone screen lit up with one new message.

Yeah. But I'd rather be there.

It was just *unfair* the way even Leo's pixels could make me smile like an idiot.

I snapped a picture of the view across my room and out of the window and sent it to him.

Well, when you're famous, we can stay in places like this all the time. I've decided I'm going to be your POD.

My what?

Tell you later. Speaking of which, can I call you earlier than we planned? This hotel is literally celebrity central – I need a pep talk in acting cool.

> You're already cool, Dyl. But about the call.

> What about it?

> Something's come up.

I stared at my phone. Those same three words again – the ones Leo had used to say he couldn't see me this half-term. I knew what they meant by now. They meant nothing. Nothing for me and Leo.

Not even a stupid phone call.

I typed something angry into my phone and made myself delete it and typed instead:

> Oh. Never mind, then.

The message vanished into the empty space between us with a whooshing sound, just as a blood-curdling scream came from outside in the hall.

FOURTEEN

'A RAT – I SAW A RAT!'

Outside our room, a little bit further along the hallway, one of the room-service porters had climbed on to the top of his silver trolley and was holding a fork and a domed serving platter out in front of him like a sword and shield.

Mum, Dad, Kayla and Jude had beaten me to investigating the noise. All along the corridor, other people were peering out of their rooms.

'It's not a rat – it's a hamster,' Jude muttered.

'IT WAS A RAT!' the porter screeched, though I didn't think he could have heard. 'HUGE AND ORANGE WITH SAUCER EYES AND SHARP, EVIL TEETH.'

'Orange?' Kayla whispered to me.

'I *know*,' I hissed back, scanning the floor in case Fluffy had escaped the food trolley and was making a beeline for the feet of any of the probably-rich-and-posh people who'd actually paid for their rooms on our floor.

In the doorway opposite ours, a young woman was clutching her baby and looking concerned. The baby wasn't fussed; just busy fiddling with a dummy that it eventually dropped on the floor.

The porter pointed to the rolling piece of plastic and shrieked. 'THERE, SEE? HELP! RAT!'

'He's clearly imagining things,' Mum said under her breath.

Jude looked round at me woefully. 'It's not a rat – it's a *hamster*.'

I put a finger to my lips to shush him – we didn't need anyone to know we'd given the hotel a *second* pest-control problem, and who knew what might happen to Fluffy if the hotel management found out he was real?

At the same time, Kayla stepped forward. She'd told me before that one of the key skills of a good lawyer is the ability to stay calm under pressure. She was clearly going to be an amazing one: she could make her voice as soothing as a lullaby.

'Hello. I'm Kayla. It's nice to meet you –' she stood on tiptoe to read the name on the porter's badge – '*Alfie*. Has it been a long shift?'

Alfie, distracted from his hyperventilating hamster-based panic, nodded slowly. 'Ten hours.'

'That *is* long,' Kayla crooned sympathetically. 'I'm sure the hot kitchens and all the fragrance and music they pump through the halls must have left you practically *dizzy* by now. Are you feeling OK?'

Alfie paused. 'I am perhaps feeling . . . a little . . . woozy?'

'And it must be easy to see a shadow and mistake it for something else?' Kayla said it as if it were an answer, not a question.

As Alfie nodded slowly, people around us started sighing and going back into their rooms. Mum and Dad moved in to help – Dad held his hands up for Alfie to take.

'If you're dizzy, you don't want to be standing up there, mate. Come on, before you have a fall.'

Alfie reached nervously to accept Dad's help at the same time as a door down the hall slammed open.

'Are those the chilli dogs? Perfect timing,' a chirpy Australian voice called.

The colour drained out of Kayla from her scalp to her fingertips. She stood still enough to be mistaken for an ice sculpture as Antoni Deathsplash, probably the best bass guitarist in the world, strolled up to slide a large silver-domed platter from between Alfie's legs.

'Cheers, man – keep the change.'

Without pausing for a second to consider what might be unusual about a porter standing on top of the dinner cart, instead of on the floor with a tray in his hand, Antoni leaned over and tucked his tip into Alfie's sock. Then he strolled back to his room, whistling.

When he reached the door, he called, 'Hey, Jenna – dinner's here!'

'Big stars eat special macrobiotic diets, don't you know,' I whispered in Kayla's ear. It was the fastest way to crack through the icy veneer and turn her skin coloured again.

'Maybe they're vegan dogs,' she huffed.

'Blue crunchy ones?'

And then she clutched my arm. 'Dylan, *look*.'

Further up the corridor, a tiny flash of orange zipped across the carpet and into the Deathsplash suite, just as the door slammed shut again.

Jude had missed it. Even more fortunately, Mum and Dad had missed it too, as Alfie picked exactly that moment to swoon delicately off the trolley and right into Mum's arms. Fortunately, as a paramedic, she was used to dragging people heavier than she was around.

She got Alfie laid out on the plush carpet while Dad knelt down to check his vitals. Then she straightened up and brushed off her hands, smartly.

'Right then. Kayla, go and call reception – let them know one of their porters is down for the count. Jude, Dylan . . .' She stopped, and lifted up a couple of the covers on the still-trollied meals. 'Well, I have no idea whether these are ours, but they'll do. Go and lay the table, will you?'

It was funny the way things you'd daydreamed about all your life never turned out quite the same way in reality. For example, when I'd imagined staying in a luxury suite and having room service delivered to my door, I'd never expected to have to carry it in myself, after loading up my little brother with a selection of knives, forks and small bowls containing salt, pepper and teeny tiny spoons (because apparently when you're posh, you're too rich to shake things on your own food).

I hadn't expected that my dream, deluxe scenario would end in my family arguing over which plate of food we didn't actually order was whose, or that by the time we'd decided on a plate and eaten, our *real* dinner would show up at the door, and I'd have to watch Dad make a valiant attempt at eating not only seconds, but thirds, fourths and fifths.

Just like when I'd dreamed about having a boyfriend, I hadn't got to the part of the dream where I never saw him, and where he even cancelled *phone* dates because everything in the whole world seemed like it was more important than me. I was trying really hard to be understanding. Whatever Leo was doing was probably really important. It was probably his big chance to show the world how brilliant he was. Just because I already knew he was brilliant, didn't mean I got to keep that secret to myself.

Maybe whatever he was doing was the thing that would shoot him to fame and make me the world's first glamorous POD.

Or maybe it wouldn't. Maybe it would turn out I wasn't even a P, after all.

After dinner (or six dinners, in Dad's case) I sloped back to my room and tossed the phone on the bed. It lit up for a moment.

There were new messages on the screen. With the whole rat crisis in the hallway, I hadn't checked to see whether Leo had replied to my never mind.

He had. The whole screen was taken up with a flood of green text boxes. I scrolled through.

Hey, I mind.

This week's been messed up enough for us already, but something really has come up.

Can't wait until I can tell you about it properly, in person.

Because, more than anything, I can't wait to see you.

> Dyl?

> Gotta go. I hope everything's OK. Hope you are.

> Xxx

Reading down the screen, the heavy lead coating around my heart slowly started to warm up and melt away.

But there was one message, at the bottom of the list, that wasn't from Leo. There was just a phone number at the top – one I didn't have listed in my contacts.

> Got your number off the team listing. Just wanted to say you were on great form today, so don't let Dutton grind you down. Looking forward to tomorrow. Fred.

Fred. I turned the letters round in my head just in case someone might have made a typo. Maybe *Fred* was what *Fauntleroy Genghis Charlemagne Hughes* autocorrected to. But no, there was only one Fred in the team – only one person even close.

Freddie Alton was looking forward to seeing me tomorrow.

FIFTEEN

Although I'd walked in with my nerves tied in more knots than my shoelaces, the second day at Feet of the Future wasn't too bad. We'd started playing some five-a-side matches, splitting up into three groups of ten, and I'd managed to avoid being on Freddie's team every time.

I didn't manage to avoid Jez Dutton's bad books, though. At lunchtime, he overheard me pointing out that Lacey Laine was reading the same copy of *MOXY Magazine* as yesterday, except this time, she was holding it upside down.

That meant twenty more laps, but more importantly it meant I didn't have to try to figure out how to use my voice box while Freddie was less than ten feet away for the whole of lunch either.

We spent the afternoon practising penalties, which are my speciality. When I played on the school team, I was always a striker – usually playing centre forward. I could be quick down the pitch and a sharpshooter by the goal. I was really good at confusing the goalie. This time, both Laurie and me tied equally for managing to get every penalty home. There were no words of praise from Jez, though. He went straight into a lecture on how there could only be eleven people on the field, and anyone he didn't think was up to scratch by the end of the week would be left on the bench for the students-versus-pro-players match on our last day.

'And you know who's captaining the pros?' Jez said, showing every single tooth in his mouth as his lips dragged up into a vicious smile. 'Me. So which of you thinks you can take me?'

Nobody replied.

Up in the stands, Lacey Laine turned the pages of ʌXOW and smiled, calling down, 'You tell 'em, babe. Jez Dutton – ten times tougher than a teenager, wooo!'

Jez smirked, and Lacey's smile vanished just a second before her head dipped behind the pages again.

'All right – tomorrow, we start looking at set pieces and choosing positions,' Jez announced, as we gathered to sign out. 'Which means today was your last chance to screw up. Tomorrow, we get serious. I mentioned there'd be scouts at this match, didn't I?'

A whisper went round the team. Chidi had been right. This was probably the last chance most of us would get to be spotted for the youth squad of a professional team. We were already nearly too old.

And I wasn't going to tell Dad anything about it. It

wasn't that I didn't think being given the chance to try out for a professional football team would be amazing, I just didn't think it was likely to happen. And I was fine with that, but Dad would have got his hopes sky high. Somehow, it's always so much worse disappointing other people than being disappointed yourself.

Anyway, it was all anyone was talking about as we shuffled through to the changing room. Freddie clapped me on the shoulder as he passed and called out, 'Great going!' loud enough that a couple of other boys turned round to look, adding comments like, 'Yeah, you're an assassin!' And, 'Well, we know who's playing up front.'

Laurie Deering scowled and said nothing.

It felt good to be noticed that way, and as I smiled at Freddie and just about managed to scratch out a, 'You too!' from the hollow of my throat, I found I had that weird guilty feeling in my stomach again.

Which was so stupid. I didn't have anything to feel guilty about. Maybe Freddie liked me a bit, but it wasn't as if he *liked* me.

Grabbing my kitbag from the peg next to Leroy's. I stripped off my shirt, and that's when I heard it.

'Pssssst.'

A soft hiss that somehow cut through the general chat. I looked around. There are two types of boys you'll meet in communal changing room. There are the ones like Freddie and Chidi who think it's totally fine and normal to have a casual chat while shirtless (or worse), and then there are the *normal* people who just want to keep as many clothes on as possible and won't make eye contact until there's no chance of someone judging their six pack (or lack of one).

I'm one of the normal ones, by the way. If I could change inside a tent, I totally would.

'Psssssssssst,' it came again – a little louder this time. But there was definitely no one on the opposite side of the bench trying to attract my attention.

I glanced behind me.

A football was floating in mid-air between where I was changing and the storeroom door.

As I watched, it lifted a few feet further into the air and jiggled frantically from side to side.

Was the training ground haunted by the ghost of a vengeful ex-pro, forever stuck doing keepy-uppies in the afterlife?

Probably not.

Squinting a bit more, I noticed a white painted stick poking out of one side of the ball, leading through to where the storeroom door was open just a crack.

Checking no one was watching me, I followed it to its source.

And found Kayla crouching behind a stack of training cones.

'What are you doing in the boys changing room?' I whispered frantically. Any moment, she'd be caught, and everyone would think I'd snuck a friend in to leer at them.

'I didn't mean to—' Kayla started.

'*While* they're changing!' I exclaimed, almost forgetting to keep my voice low. 'I haven't even got a shirt on!'

I crossed my arms over my chest.

'Dylan, when we were twelve, you spent a whole year making me tell you if I thought your muscles had grown at least once a week. I think we're past the *coy about your boy-boobs* stage.' Kayla folded her own arms, probably for a different reason.

'They are *not* boy-boobs,' I huffed. 'What are you doing here, then?'

'I needed supplies for my next challenge. I have to make a video of a haunting – so I thought, why not film it here? I just need to borrow a few of these cones and balls and alter them first.'

'Alter them?'

She nodded. 'You know, make a few holes, add a few extras so they'll move on their own. I was thinking of adding wheels to some of the cones.'

I shook my head. 'If you start putting balls on sticks and making holes in things, it's not like you can give them back. That doesn't sound much like borrowing to me.'

'No – it sounds like *stealing*,' a voice said from the back of the storeroom. Rising from under a vaulting horse like an avenging angel, his yellow ringlets still dripping shower water on to his shoulders, emerged Leroy. 'And not only is that against the law; it could get you kicked off the course.'

SIXTEEN

'I'm not *on* any course,' Kayla was arguing, forgetting to keep her voice to an appropriate hiding-in-a-cupboard level no matter how much I *shhh*-ed her.

'Then what *are* you doing here?' Leroy demanded, trying not to drop the towel that he'd draped around himself like a fluffy Roman toga. 'I think you'll find trespassing is also generally frowned upon by the relevant authorities.'

'Well, aren't you clever. So far, you've let me know both burglary and trespassing are illegal. How incredible – I never knew.' I could tell Kayla was getting really snippy now. She only used this trick of repeating things back at people when she was about to demonstrate how stupid they were. 'Fortunately, now I'll be able to call you as witness if I plead ignorance in a court of law.'

'Will you both please *stop*?' I stepped in between them, trying not to cut myself on the daggers they were staring at each other. 'Leroy, Kayla *is* booked on to a course. She's just not . . . actually doing it.'

'Why not?' he asked suspiciously.

'Ethical reasons,' said Kayla, adopting a haughty air.

'I object to cheerleaders being considered anything other than elite athletes deserving of their own events, not just being a sideshow to yours.'

'I thought you objected to cheerleaders?' I asked, feeling like I must have missed something somewhere.

'Well, I did,' Kayla admitted. 'But I watched some of their sessions today and changed my mind. They're actually really incredible, and cheerleading's so much more interesting than football. It also has a *much* better soundtrack. Anyway, the *point is* I have a legal premise for being in the building.'

'Sounds more like a case of fraud and deception to me,' Leroy retorted.

I put my head in my hands. 'You're not actually helping things here.'

Leroy did a great job of looking mortally wounded. Seriously, if the sports didn't work out, he could go into theatre instead. He looked a bit like those portraits of miserable children you had to look at when you studied Shakespeare and the Tudors.

'I'm not *planning* to help this – this – *friend* of yours abscond with team equipment. For one thing, I don't know what sort of video you think you're going to make, but I accidentally got locked in here for three hours after practice yesterday, and I'm almost completely certain it's not *haunted*.'

Taking a shaky breath, Leroy turned to throw a nervous glance into the dimly lit cupboard behind him, suggesting the *almost* was more important than the *certain*. I was about to ask how he'd got locked in, and why he'd decided to come back in here again after the clearly traumatic experience, when he went on – glaring at me.

'And for another, I might expect this of someone so . . . alternative-looking.' As Kayla squeaked indignantly at this description, Leroy held up a hand and whispered loudly to me from behind it, '*Sorry – it's the hair.*' Then he continued, 'But, Dylan, I wouldn't have expected it from *you*. After our talk yesterday, I thought we trusted each other.'

Now Kayla was looking confused, probably wondering why I'd neglected to share whatever soul-baring experience Leroy and I had here yesterday. She hadn't really met him properly at Starcross Sands. He'd been the quietest one in the gang he hung out with, and even I'd only really spoken to him when we'd played football.

I could see her squinting at him now, though. 'Do I know you from somewhere?'

Leroy attempted to look mysterious. 'We do have a history. I know your past. I know what you did last summer.'

'Oh, for goodness sake.' I sighed. 'Kayla, he was at Starcross Sands with us. The only history he knows is that your hair used to be pink.'

'*Very alternative,*' Leroy muttered.

'Leroy, nobody's stealing any balls,' I said, firmly. Then I added, firmer still, 'Kayla, *nobody's* stealing any balls. We'll just have to figure out another way to get some props for your video.'

'Maybe I can help?'

Freddie Alton's voice came from a couple of inches behind my left ear, so soft and so warm and so *unexpected* that I almost did a somersault over the vaulting horse in surprise.

Somehow managing to keep on my feet, I tripped over my words instead, turning towards him to coolly reply, 'I . . . Uh. I – I? Um.'

Really, I didn't know how I hadn't already been scouted as a live-TV presenter or hot upcoming DJ, given my flawless ability to stay smooth and keep talking under pressure.

Kayla was already beaming and holding out a hand in Freddie's direction. He blinked at it a couple of times before realizing she wanted to shake.

'Freddie!' She greeted him like they were best friends. She didn't even put that much warmth in her voice when she said *my* name, and we'd been inseparable for years. 'Kayla Flores – you might know me as captain of the school's cheer squad. I'm here with Dylan – sorry, I didn't have a chance to say hello to you at the hotel.'

Freddie's eyebrows lifted, and I could see him trying to place something. Most people at school knew Kayla by sight at least, because being eye-catching was number seven on her list of daily goals – it must have been something else he couldn't figure out.

'Does the school *have* a cheer squad?' he asked, finally. He looked a little guilty, since being sports captain and not knowing that would have been a bit of an oversight.

If anything, Kayla's flashbulb beam of a smile grew wider. 'It does next term. As well as being captain, I should have mentioned I'm also the founder member.'

Freddie's expression cracked into a smile. 'Ah, I see. And you know the sports captain has to sign off on any new teams?'

'I do,' Kayla said conspiratorially. 'But we'll talk about that later. You said you could help me with my video?'

She looked around the storage cupboard. 'I'm not sure how. My idea was to make it look as though these were being kicked around the hallway by invisible players, but *somebody* won't let me borrow them, and no one's going to have five or six spare footballs just sitting around at home.'

'Actually . . .' Freddie started.

'Jez might,' Leroy put in helpfully. 'Of course, he hates Dylan and would probably hate anyone associated with Dylan. But we could always get someone he doesn't openly despise to ask him.'

'*Thanks*,' I said, not looking at Freddie. It was obvious Jez wasn't my biggest fan, but I didn't exactly want to be known as the rubbish one who spent every day doing enforced laps forever.

'Well, that's an option,' Freddie said awkwardly. 'But I was going to say, actually my mum has. Not at home, though – in our hotel room.'

That was so weird, it actually startled me into speaking to him, even if it was just to repeat what he'd said like a startled parrot. 'Your mum has footballs in your hotel room?'

Freddie nodded. 'But not five or six.'

Kayla, who'd started to look hopeful, let out a sigh.

'More like fifty or sixty.'

We *all* turned into startled parrots, then.

'Your mum—' Leroy started.

'Has *sixty footballs*,' Kayla cut in.

'In your hotel room?' I finished. 'Why?'

Freddie shuffled his feet, looking as embarrassed as he had back in the hotel lobby when we first arrived. It was weird to see the way he started to fold in on himself, as though being smaller made a person less noticeable.

Kayla was four foot ten and should have been obvious evidence that wasn't the case.

'You know there's a celebration dinner and trophy presentation back at the hotel after the students versus pros match on Friday?' We all nodded. Freddie shrugged. 'Well, Mum offered to decorate. There's going to be a bit of a theme.'

Kayla and Leroy were still looking dumbstruck, but before I even realized it, I was nodding sympathetically.

'Dad heard about that. He's still upset they didn't want to let him DJ for it – he was going to do his special singalong set of World Cup team anthems, all night long.'

Freddie shot me a quick smile, almost as if he was grateful for me sharing one of my weird dad stories to counter his weird mum. It made me feel so warm and squishy inside, I started to worry my internal organs were liquefying.

'And your mum wouldn't miss a few?' Kayla guessed.
Freddie nodded.

'Oh, you're a *lifesaver*. That's *brilliant*.'

She pulled out a notebook from her skirt pocket. 'Right, well, if you'd all like to put some clothes on, I'm going to head down the hall and plan my shoot.'

She turned to edge past Freddie through the storeroom

door as a pale, slightly damp hand clamped over her shoulder.

'No you don't. There's no way I'm leaving you alone now we know your previous criminal intentions. We might get out and find the whole hall gone.'

Kayla shot Leroy a withering look. 'Unless I've got a bulldozer in my pocket, it seems unlikely.'

'Well, *who knows* . . .' Leroy exclaimed, frogmarching Kayla towards the door.

Leaving me and Freddie in the changing room. Alone.

Just as my phone started to ring.

Leo.

SEVENTEEN

The thing about phones is they're supposed to be private. They're personal, portable, pocket-sized prisons for all the little secrets you really don't want anyone else to know.

For example, if you google *Tom Holland Spider-Man arms*, your mum might sit down at the family computer one evening, decide to look up *tomahawk* to help with a crossword clue, and accidentally find it. And then, if she happens to be really, really immature about it, she might start using the *Spider-Man* theme tune as the soundtrack to her morning exercise routine, shooting you knowing looks while doing bicep curls holding tins of store-brand beans.

Google *Tom Holland Spider-Man arms* on your *phone*, and no one will ever know. They won't even know if you've googled *How to get Tom Holland Spider-Man arms if I'm too lazy to work out* or *How can someone look so gorgeous squatting in a primary-coloured onesie please advise* or *I even fancy him with the mask on, do I need professional help?*

Even if you've got your own laptop, there's no guarantee of privacy. Someone might ask to borrow it, and if you say yes, they might stumble into that one folder where you saved an epic multi-part fan fiction about a dead *Harry Potter* character. And if you say *no*, they might start to suspect you have weird secret folders anyway. Maybe even weird secret folders about dead *Harry Potter* characters where they get to stay alive and fall in love with other *Harry Potter* characters, while working part time in a coffee shop, and owning a cat called Frisky.

There's just no way to win.

It's also true that someone might ask to borrow your phone. But there's an unspoken rule, which dictates that phones can only be borrowed to make calls with, because everyone *knows* all the other bits are full of secrets. So then if you spot them looking something up online, or trying to scroll through the last two hundred selfies you took (where you'd been trying to get just one where the light falling across your face made you look tanned and mature and even a little bit like you might finally be growing stubble, rather than just lurking ominously in someone's bathroom in the dark like a baby-faced serial killer), then you'd have every right to cut them out of your life forever. No one would think that wasn't reasonable behaviour.

But the problem with how safe phones *seem* is that you start to get lulled into a false sense of security.

It's way too easy to forget that the photo that flashes up every time your boyfriend calls happens to be covered in little animated hearts, and that you'd let your best friend add a dashing floral crown to the top of his head for 'effect'.

Or that the ringtone you'd set for him was 'Crazy in Love'.

I'd never hung up on Leo before, but as Freddie Alton looked between me and my phone with a curious expression, I did it without even hesitating.

And that didn't help anything at all.

Because the next thing Freddie asked was obvious. Inevitable, even.

'Who was that?'

And even though I was waiting for it, I had no idea what to say.

It wasn't down to the usual tongue-tied feeling I got around Freddie. It wasn't that I was going to trip over the words if I said them. It's that words weren't even going to get a chance to make it out through the desert dryness of my mouth. My throat suddenly felt like someone had filled it with sandpaper.

The worst part was, I knew why I felt like that, and I'd thought I was over it. It was fear. The really specific fear that comes from knowing that, any minute, someone's going to find out something new about you, and it might just change the way they look at you forever.

That's what happens when you tell people you're gay. *Most* people are fine with it, if you're lucky – it never changed anything with Kayla, or with Mum and Dad, even if it took me ages to get up the courage to say anything to them. And with a few people at school starting to find out now, I hadn't really noticed any of them treating me differently. There might have been a couple of things said behind my back, but that was true for basically everyone. Maybe that just made me normal.

Because being gay *is* normal. I know that. I know there's nothing weirder or worse about fancying someone whose anatomy diagram appears on the same page of the biology textbook as your own than there is fancying someone whose diagram's in a whole different chapter. It would be strange, wouldn't it, to think that love was a good thing, but only if you were anatomical opposites below the waist. We've all got the same kind of hearts, after all.

But people are strange – that's the thing. I'd had a few comments since people started finding out, but they didn't usually bother me much. Kayla says that people who bully others for being different are either ignorant or they're scared someone will find out they're different too, and I think she's probably right.

But Freddie had been really nice to me so far, even

if half our conversations had involved me nodding silently or faking a medical condition to explain my vocal malfunction.

And he was smart, and talented, and had arm muscles that . . . were definitely, completely unimportant when it came to my opinion about his opinion of me.

I just really would have liked him to like me, that was all. And wanting that made facing the moment when things might be about to change a little bit harder.

But Freddie was waiting for an answer to who was calling, and I didn't know how to lie and not feel like I'd let down either Leo or myself, somehow.

So coughing the Sahara out of my throat, I said the simplest, most honest thing I could manage.

'Oh, he's called Leo.'

Freddie had already started walking away from me, grabbing a shirt from his kitbag and pulling it over his head. That should have made it easier for me to concentrate around him, but it didn't, really.

He grinned. 'That doesn't tell me much. Is he from school?'

'No, I – um. I met him on holiday. He's a ballet dancer – he's going to be famous for it one day.'

For a minute, I almost started to give a nostalgic lecture on the delights of Starcross Sands and its crazy manager and chemical toilets, and the way Nibbles the dancing hamster had been the star attraction in the place. Just the memory of Leo in that stupid furry outfit made me smile.

But Freddie was frowning over something. 'Isn't ballet for girls?'

And my brain immediately translated the question as, 'Isn't ballet a bit gay?'

If I'd been asked that a while ago, I might have laughed it off and tried to find a way to avoid answering that, no, dancing isn't a bit gay. And nor is hairdressing, or fashion design. In fact, no jobs are a bit gay; it's just that some gay people happen to do them.

And if that was all it took, it would make football 'a bit gay' too. I was proof of that.

Besides, I'd seen Leo dance, and he was incredible, and I was totally sure that had nothing to do with whether he fancied boys or girls.

'Actually, dancers are proper endurance athletes. Did you know there are more injuries in dancing than football? Their pain tolerance is incredible. You should see the state of Leo's feet. In fact . . .' I grabbed my phone and scrolled through the photos I'd marked as favourites until I got to what Kayla always told me was the weirdest one.

It was a picture of Leo's feet. Only his feet, from the ankles down. They were bruised and strapped up, like they'd been in a bar fight with six pairs of angry DM boots. I thought it was amazing he could still walk like that.

I showed Freddie, who whistled. 'Blimey. But, why do you keep a picture of someone's feet on your phone?'

Which was a really good question. And I didn't have an answer ready at all. 'I, um. I just like feet? I mean I don't *like feet* like feet. Not in a weird, hanging around Foot Locker smelling the shoehorns kind of way. It's just his feet I like. Well –' I took a long, deep breath – 'I like all of him.'

Freddie's eyes widened for a moment. 'Oh. Is he . . . your boyfriend, then?'

And even though I'd already almost said it myself, it startled me to hear him use that description out loud, like it was so simple.

It's just not a leap that people make often. No one assumes I've got a boyfriend until I tell them, even though people assume Kayla's my girlfriend all the time. So for some reason, when Freddie did, it felt almost nice. Like a little bit of the pressure that was settling round my shoulders had eased off.

It made it much simpler to just nod, catching myself smiling a little, helplessly, as I confirmed it properly for him. 'Sort of. Mostly. I think. Yeah.'

I was still waiting for something to change. Something

tiny and almost imperceptible at the corner of Freddie's eyes, maybe. Some sort of sneer.

It didn't happen. Not at all.

Although I suppose I could have missed it, because all the stress meant I somehow got my arm through the collar of my shirt and spent a minute trying to shove my head out through my armpit before figuring out the mistake.

Freddie was dressed when I emerged from the shirt, his kitbag slung over one shoulder, like a model from a sports catalogue. He looked like he'd been waiting for me to break up the fight with my own clothes before he replied.

He smiled.

And then he said, 'That's a shame.'

That heavy weight fell from my shoulders right into the pit of my stomach. 'Look, if you've got some kind of problem with it, then—'

He held up a hand, shaking his head. 'No, no – I mean it's a shame you've got a boyfriend already, that's all. Because I think you're kind of cute.'

And then he was gone, heading through the changing-room doors. And even though I was standing still, for a minute it felt like everything was spinning.

EIGHTEEN

I was still feeling a bit dizzy about what Freddie had said when Kayla stuck her head around the door and sighed at me. 'If you haven't got any trousers on in two minutes, you're going to have to risk arrest for indecent exposure. We're about to miss the bus.'

I chucked on the last of my clothes and sprinted for the bus stop, emerging from the training centre into the kind of rain that takes two seconds to soak you right through from your coat to your pants. I could have brought a towel with me and had my shower right there.

Ahead of me, a bright red sports car had pulled half up on to the pavement. You'd think Jez Dutton might have wanted to drive something more subtle after the whole curry-crash incident, but apparently not. And there, sashaying her way towards the car, was Lacey Laine.

She could afford to sashay, despite the rain, because she had Laurie and Chidi on either side of her holding umbrellas over her head. They were both soaked, but not a single feather on Lacey's marabou mules had so much as wilted in the rain. I skidded to a stop for a moment, watching her climb in beside Jez and wave her helpers goodbye.

They stood there, dazed and dripping.

I only realized I was doing the same thing when I heard my name yelled across the tarmac and looked up to see Kayla standing between the front doors of the bus.

She was busily pretending to be the world's slowest person while getting her bus ticket out, fumbling around for it in the bottom of her oversized bag, when I slammed in through the doors behind her.

It was the same driver we'd had yesterday. He didn't look all that pleased to see me, but Kayla turned her head and grinned, gasping suddenly and patting her jacket pocket.

'Well, what do you know? It was in here *the whole time.*' She showed the driver her weekly pass and smiled sweetly. 'Thank you for your patience.'

I dug out my soggy, disintegrating one and held that up too, as he grunted and nodded me past.

'Was that—' Kayla began, picking two seats at the back.

'Lacey Laine? Yup.' I nodded, sitting and trying to ruffle the water out of my hair with my fingertips. It didn't help much. 'She's been here the last two days. No idea why. I don't think I'd want to spend all my time watching *us* play football – even if I didn't have three perfume sponsorship deals and a black Nando's card – but it seems like she does.'

'Maybe she just doesn't have much else to do,' Kayla suggested. 'Do you think she'll come in tomorrow?'

'I don't know – probably. What are you smiling at?'

'Nothing. I'm not smiling!' Kayla protested, grinning like the Grinch surrounded by stolen Christmas presents. 'I've just had an idea for making my video go a bit more viral, that's all.'

I should probably have been suspicious about that, but I was too busy trying to dry off my wet phone on my wet shirt and heaving a massive sigh of relief when it still turned on despite its smeary, damp surface.

Three missed calls. Since I'd cut him off while I was talking to Freddie, Leo had tried to get in touch with me three more times.

Something in my chest felt uncomfortably tight as I swiped the call notifications away. I should have been pleased that he'd made so much effort. He must have really wanted to talk to me. But I'd picked talking to someone else instead.

What if Leo started thinking *I* was the one who wasn't interested any more? He hadn't left any messages. What if four calls were his limit, and now he'd realized he was wasting his time trying to reach me and had gone to spend time with some of the other dancers he was rehearsing with?

I tried to picture them, but my knowledge of what dancers must look like was mostly based around Leo. Which made them all really tall, and fit, and stupidly good-looking, with wide smiles and kind eyes. I hated them all already. Worst of all, *they* weren't halfway across the country from him being made to run laps by Satan's favourite football coach.

I should definitely have picked ballet instead of football when we were offered after-school sports in primary school.

'Dylan?'

'After all, pirouettes can't be that different from three-sixty-degree spins, right?'

Kayla blinked at me for a moment. 'I honestly have no idea. But maybe you can ask Leo, if you answer your phone.'

I'd turned the sound off, somehow, but she pointed to where the picture of Leo with his love hearts and floral crown was lighting up the screen in my lap. I don't know how I'd possibly felt embarrassed about it. It was the best picture *ever*.

The call asked me if I wanted to connect with video. I tapped on yes, and Leo's face – his real, right-now, not-out-with-a-bunch-of-stupid-sexy-dancers face – was right there.

I didn't even care that I could feel how hard Kayla was rolling her eyes at my goofy smile.

'Hi.'

Even better, Leo was smiling too.

'Hey, I thought I was going to miss you.' He pauses, squinting a little at the screen. *'Were you in the bath?'*

'Oh, no.' I looked at the little picture of myself in the corner of the screen, alerting me to the way my hair was slicked down across my forehead like a shiny black swimming cap. Really attractive. I tried to ruffle it up again, but only managed to slick it backwards, now looking like a greasy gangster from a mafia movie. 'The rain. You rang while I was running for the bus.'

I tipped my screen so Leo could see Kayla in the window seat beside me, rain still hammering against the glass. 'See?'

It was only a little lie. He *had* rung while I was running for the bus. At least, the second or third time.

'I see,' Leo's voice said, the phone still tipped away. *'Hi, Kayla. Dylan told me you were cheerleading.'*

Kayla waved at my phone. 'That's also what I told Dylan I was doing.'

'Uh-huh. So what are you doing instead?'

Pulling my arm back, I gaped at Leo. 'You've met

121

Kayla, like, three times! How did you know?'

Leo grinned. *'I've met Kayla three times. It's enough. So what's she doing?'*

Kayla leaned over. 'I'm mounting an assault on the monolith of rock.'

'So trying to win some Deathsplash tickets?' Leo nodded. *'Cool.'*

My mouth still hadn't closed since the cheerleading thing. I glared at Kayla. 'Did you give him some kind of Kayla-to-English translation book you've never told me about?'

On-screen, Leo was laughing. It was kind of the best sound ever. *'No, I just saw this thing linked on Twitter this morning. "Ten Crazy Ways Fans Are Trying to Win Concert Tickets." One of them was this photo of some cute boy in a chicken shop, half covered by a sheet and looking like he'd got mugged by a ketchup-wielding maniac. It had Kayla's handle under it.'*

Kayla clutched my arm. 'I made the top ten! That has to be a good sign.'

'You thought I looked cute?' I asked Leo, feeling the tops of my ears starting to get warm enough to evaporate off the rain.

'Cute and ketchuppy,' Leo said.

'It was hot sauce. I'm still finding it in unsavoury places.' I sighed. 'So what are you doing?'

'*Rehearsals are tough,*' Leo replied. '*And boring. Not much to report.*' He glanced at his watch. '*I'd better go, though – we've got this thing tonight.*'

'Thing?' I raised my eyebrows.

Was it my imagination, or did he look guilty for a moment?

'*Going out,*' he said, '*with some of the other dancers. Anyway, it was good to see your face. Dry off safely, yeah?*'

I was still nodding dumbly when he hung up. I hated every single one of Leo's fellow dancers' gorgeous, imaginary faces.

'What do you think he meant, dry off safely?' I asked Kayla, finally.

'Well, you have been known to headbutt hand dryers before,' she muttered, but she'd stopped paying any real attention when Leo had mentioned her photo. She held her own phone up now, triumphant.

We really had made the pages of a few news websites talking about the contest. Two photos of me seemed to be the main image for all the articles: one in a ghostly sheet, flying through the air in a shower of chick'n bits; the other lying on the pavement with the sheet pulled away from my face and wrapped round me like a shroud.

'Look, we have to win now – we're famous!' Kayla declared. 'You're a celebrity spook now, Dylan.'

The bus turned into the hotel car park, and I peered past her out of the window.

'Speaking of spooks . . . please tell me that's not what Mum's looking for right now?'

NINETEEN

Mum was *definitely* out looking for the hotel ghost. As Kayla and I joined her outside the lobby doors, she cupped a hand around the candle she was holding and whispered, 'Is there anybody there?'

'Just us, Mum,' I said, tapping her on the shoulder. 'But there's a coachload of grannies heading this way, if you want to talk to someone historical.'

Mum jumped, startled, and turned our way. 'Dylan! Don't interrupt me like that. I'm sure I sensed something – there's a strange variance in the temperature out here.'

'You mean, where the automatic doors keep opening and letting out warm air into the cold?' I asked. 'Very spooky.'

'Dismiss it all you like,' Mum said, 'but I think there's something to it. You know, I *am* spiritually sensitive.'

'You mean you've seen ghosts?' Kayla asked.

I groaned. It was always a bad idea to engage Mum on this kind of thing.

Mum looked ecstatic to be asked. '*Well*, never actually *seen*,' she said in her most dramatic voice. 'But when our little cat Curly passed on, I *often* heard crunching

125

noises when I was alone in the kitchen . . .' She paused for effect. 'Like someone eating Friskies from beyond the grave!'

'Well, there *are* famous cases of animal ghosts,' Kayla said.

I rolled my eyes and tried to hiss something about not encouraging Mum, but she'd already launched into her story.

'For example, the Demon Cat of Washington DC is very well known,' Kayla went on, while Mum nodded, as if this were total stone-clad proof that she was a pet psychic. 'It's been seen for hundreds of years in the hallways of the government buildings there. They say it appears at times of great change, like election days and political tragedies. It was seen before the assassinations of Lincoln *and* Kennedy.'

'Don't you think there's a chance it might just be . . . a cat?' I asked. 'I see cats all the time. And how do they know it's the same one anyway? I don't mean to be catist, but they all look the same to me.'

Kayla smiled, looking like someone who should be telling this story under a blanket by a camp fire, with a torch held under their chin. 'Because *this* cat grows bigger and bigger when someone approaches it, until it's the size of a tiger with pitch-black fur. They say it pounces on unsuspecting intruders, vanishing seconds before its giant teeth would close round their throat.'

'See, Dylan – I *told* you I had paranormal abilities.' Mum looked as pleased as the giant demon cat that got the cream.

'So who died and made you the physical embodiment of Wikipedia?' I asked Kayla, after we'd left Mum wondering if Mary the ghostly maid might have a few spectral pets.

'Actually, I *am* an editor for them,' Kayla retorted, tossing her head. 'I read about a project someone started to add more female scientists to the listings, and I decided to start my own, dedicated to female lawyers. Although they did delete one of my suggestions, because it turns out Reese Witherspoon didn't *really* go to law school.'

When we got out of the hotel lift, Kayla took up her now habitual position next to me on the opposite side of the hall to the set of rooms we now knew belonged to the Deathsplash Nightmares. It was weird to have her use me to hide behind. I was usually the one with the irrational anxieties.

'They're probably out doing publicity or something,' I told her. 'I don't think rock stars spend whole weeks just sitting around in their hotel rooms.'

Unlike us. Dad and Jude were at the cinema, but I

wasn't invited so I could 'rest my goal-scoring feet'. I had no idea why I couldn't do that in front of a big screen while stuffing my face with popcorn.

'And I still don't know why you're not staking out their room like you're MI5 and they're Britain's most wanted,' I continued, stopping outside the room we'd seen Antoni Deathsplash emerge from to see if I could tell whether the lights were on in there. 'Any of the other fans outside would be.'

The huge crowd of people from our first day was gone, since the hotel had taken to sending security guards out to disperse it, but there were usually still a few hopefuls loitering around.

Kayla made a strange, strangled sort of sound and dragged on my shirt to try and get me to move away from the door. 'That's just it. I don't *want* to be "any other fan". If I can win this contest, I'll have proved my talent and commitment. I'll be meeting them as an equal, not just some fangirl who snuck into the hotel.'

Lots of people *were* trying to do that. We'd been woken up by loud shrieks as security tried to remove a girl who'd packed herself in a box addressed to Rick Deathsplash and had it delivered to reception by a bike courier. Unfortunately the porter had dropped her on the way out of the lift and realized something was up when his parcel started swearing at him.

I heard it had been Alfie, the same porter who thought he'd seen a rat. He was looking like he might have to take early retirement soon on account of his nerves.

'All right, all right – I suppose that's a reasonable point.' I let Kayla drag me along by the back of my shirt, still trying to see if there were any signs of life down the hallway. 'But for the record, I don't think you could come across as an *average* fan even if you tried. You're not an average *anything*.'

I also wasn't sure exactly how knowing she'd taken the best photo of a chicken-eating ghost would mean one of the world's most famous rock bands would see her as an equal, but I wasn't going to say that. Arguing with Kayla and *losing* an argument with Kayla were basically the same thing. There was no point starting one unless you were prepared to do the other.

'That's very sweet, Dylan,' Kayla told me, patting me down for the key card to the room.

'Yeah, well. I mean you're not an average height, for a start.'

She glared (up) at me.

'Quit while you're ahead.'

Letting go of my shirt, she opened the door to the suite, and I sighed. Dad had obviously been doing some unpacking. The once pristine, glamorous room now looked like the terraces of Woking FC. There was even a banner with my name on it hung over the window.

Kayla looked back at me. 'At least he doesn't have a load of spare footballs.'

I thought of Freddie's mum, and the competitive look Dad got in his eyes whenever she was around. 'He doesn't *yet*.'

'Well, at least we've still got the big-screen TV.' Kayla headed over to grab the remote while I rummaged around for some of the crisps Mum had bought to keep us from raiding the minibar. 'What about having a movie night of our own?'

'We could. It's nearly Halloween – I think I'm in the mood for a horror.'

Kayla was flicking through listings already. The horror section was huge. 'What kind?'

'How about something with an evil football coach? One who forces his team to run laps around the pitch until their legs fall off.'

She looked at me curiously. 'Interesting plot. Does it have a happy ending?'

'Sort of,' I told her. 'Just when he thinks he's won, his tortured players pick up their lost limbs and come after him to beat him to death with them. The film ends with him trapped in the storage cupboard, with the ominous sound of hopping just outside.'

'Uh-huh.' Kayla abruptly flicked off the Halloween-film selection and started scrolling through cartoons for under-tens instead.

'On second thoughts, I think we should watch something with a more positive message. And you should tell me *exactly* what's going on at Feet of the Future.'

TWENTY

I tossed a packet of spicy tomato Snaps into Kayla's outstretched hand, then slouched down on to the massive white couch beside her. It was amazing how quickly you could get used to things. When we first walked into the room, I'd thought this sofa was the most incredible thing ever – too big to even fit in our living room at home. Now I was thinking about how impractical it was to have a white couch when you liked bright orange crisps.

'What do you mean, "What's going on at Feet of the Future?"' I asked. 'It's a football camp. Football's going on. Well, some football. A bit of football. Mostly played by other people.'

I rammed a handful of crisps into my mouth, a crunchy way of indicating that that was all I had to say on the matter. Meanwhile, Kayla folded her arms across her chest and stared at me with an eyebrow raised – it was only a matter of time before I caved.

'I don't think Jez Dutton likes me very much.'

'Oh, Dylan.' Kayla tutted. 'What have you done to make the Korma Calamity take against you?'

I couldn't help looking indignant. That was the problem: I didn't have an answer to give. 'I don't *know*. I haven't really done anything wrong, but I can't get anything right, either. I'm pretty sure he had me running laps just for breathing in a way he didn't like this morning. He'll be giving them out for existing soon.'

I'd told myself I didn't care what Jez thought and didn't care what position he gave me for the match, either. But looking up at the homemade banner with my name on it that Dad had draped over the curtains, I suddenly didn't think I could bear to be stuck at the back of the pitch at the end of the week, when we both knew I played best up front. He'd be so disappointed.

And I did love football. Even if it wasn't what I wanted to be doing this week – even if the way I loved football was really different to the way I thought I might be starting to love Leo – I still *loved* it. I was good at it too. Jez would have known that if he'd only let me have a proper chance to play.

Kayla looked sympathetic. 'That's terrible. And I thought your biggest athletic problem was going to be tripping over your own tongue every time Freddie Alton arrived on the pitch.'

I almost choked on a spicy Snap. 'What do you *mean*?'

'Dylan, you've fancied him for forever. And your

133

voice went up three octaves when we were talking to him in the storage cupboard today.'

'It did *not*.'

She nodded sadly. 'It did. It was like you'd been possessed by Miss Piggy.'

I let my head drop, slowly, into my tomatoey palms.

Great. I'd finally managed to have an almost normal conversation with Freddie Alton and had probably sounded like I'd been smacked between the legs by somebody's spiked boot. That's probably why he'd called me cute: cute like a Muppet.

Kayla reached across to ruffle my hair. 'It could be worse. You could have a crush on that awful Chortlefoy.'

'Fauntleroy,' I corrected. 'And he goes by Ler—'

'He's *terrible*,' she went on loudly. 'I've never *met* anyone so pedantic, so consumed by rules and facts. I don't know how you can bear him, honestly.'

I looked at her for a moment. This morning, she'd given the whole breakfast buffet a lecture about how most cereals that claimed to be 'heart healthy' actually removed all the nutrition from their food during the manufacturing process, only to shove in a load of vitamins and minerals that shouldn't naturally be there. She asked us to tweet cereal companies asking why they didn't cite scientific sources for their claims on the front of the box.

'Yeah,' I said. 'Who knows. Anyway, maybe it's better if Freddie thinks I've wandered off the set of the next Muppets movie.'

'Why would that be better?' Kayla asked.

I thought that was stupidly obvious. 'Well. Because *Leo*.'

She looked blank. 'What does your Muppet voice have to do with Leo? You don't sound like that with him – you never have.'

'No, but . . . I think my voice gets like that because I *fancy* Freddie. It's like your pop-star paralysis. Fit boys fry my vocal chords.'

'And?'

I couldn't understand how she was missing the issue here. She wanted to be a *lawyer*; they were supposed to be *smart*. 'And if I want to be with Leo, I can't just go around fancying other people, can I?'

'Oh,' Kayla said, blinking. 'Yes you can.'

'*Exactly*, it's a total betrayal – what?'

'I said, yes you can. People don't develop a blind spot for everyone else with a nice-looking face just because they've started dating someone. You've fancied Freddie *forever*. Being with Leo doesn't mean you get a switch to turn all that off. You can like someone and still like other people. Deciding to date someone just means you like them most.'

I was pretty new to dating anybody, but this wasn't something I'd thought about before. And I spent loads of time thinking about my relationship – I couldn't figure out how I'd missed it. 'Isn't it a bit like cheating, though?'

Kayla popped a crisp into her mouth and kept her lips sealed until it had melted, before replying. 'Not unless you actually cheat. You can't help noticing when other people have nice faces, Dylan. Everybody does it. Even Leo.'

Even Leo.

I thought about the line-up of imaginary other dancers I'd spent most of last night creating in my head, and instead of feeling better about what Kayla was telling me, I felt much, much worse.

She finally pressed play on the cartoon she'd picked out – something pastel and syrupy, with a gang of bears who apparently really, really cared about each other. I shook my head though, hauling myself off the couch for more snack supplies.

'I think we should go back to the horror section. I don't want to spend the whole cartoon wondering which bear I sounded most like today.'

'OK, so maybe Miss Piggy was a *slight* exaggeration...' Kayla twisted round to look at me.

'No, trust me, I want to be completely terrified

tonight.' I leaned against a stool.

And then leaped right over it, and almost out of my skin, as the door slammed open right behind me.

Mum was in the doorway, looking like she'd seen—

'A GHOST! Dylan! Kayla! Quick! Bring your cameras! I've spotted something horrific just down the hall.'

'We're on the same floor as the Deathsplash Nightmares,' I reminded her. 'Are you sure it wasn't just a rock star wearing too much eyeliner?'

Kayla looked worried for a moment, but as Mum waved her hands and hissed, 'It's nothing like that. Quick! Quick!' we both got out our phones and followed her into the dimly lit hallway.

That's when, ahead of us, I spotted a small, white runaway napkin careering at breakneck speed towards the lifts.

'There – see? A poltergeist!' Mum exclaimed, grabbing my phone to take a video. 'An undeniable spiritual entity!'

'It's that flipping hamster,' Kayla whispered to me. She stretched out a leg and tapped her foot on the edge of the napkin as it flew past.

Fluffy bolted into the lift, while the white cloth fluttered gently and then wilted to the floor.

I looked up to find Mum tapping furiously at my

phone. 'What's wrong with this? There's something blocking the image. Spiritual interference?'

'I think it's more likely to be your finger,' I said gently, reaching to change the way she held the phone. 'Did you just miss all that?'

'All what?' she asked, pressing record on the camera and holding it up now it just showing her some vague pinkish darkness. 'Now, where did the spirit go?'

'Um—' Kayla started.

'It—' I cut in.

'*Oh, it changed forms,*' Mum interrupted, bending down to pick up the napkin.

'Worse than that – it changed *floors*,' I whispered bleakly to Kayla. 'We'll never find Fluffy now.'

TWENTY-ONE

Thankfully Kayla told Jude about our strange encounter of the Fluffy kind after breakfast the next morning, otherwise all Mum's talk about pet ghosts might have put him right off his Coco Pops.

She was still going on about it when she and Dad dropped us off at Feet of the Future the next morning.

'And on top of *that*, I heard strange splashing noises in our suite last night,' she announced theatrically.

'Dad flooded the shower last night,' I pointed out. 'The splashing noises were him trying to wring out his pants.'

Mum just grinned and winked at me. Then she blinked, pointing out of the window on my side. 'Goodness, that boy's got a lot of balls.'

Kayla and I looked round to see what she meant, assuming someone must have been doing something really confident, or dangerous. Which would have been unusual for eight thirty in the morning, when most people are just dragging themselves to wherever they need to be, like zombies running low on brains.

But it was Freddie Alton, busily dragging a huge net

of footballs across the car park. He was wearing a hoody in a shade of Superman-blue that made his hair gleam gold in the early morning light. I swallowed hard and willed my voice out of Muppet territory.

'We'd better go and help him,' I growled.

'Do you need a cough sweet?' Mum asked, rustling in her bag. But I was already halfway out of the car.

'You might want to aim for somewhere *between* Mickey Mouse and Darth Vader,' Kayla commented, catching me up. 'Swinging from one to the other gets a bit confusing.'

'Very funny. Just . . . kick me if I get too squeaky, all right?' I held up a hand, waving to Freddie as we approached. Something about seeing him still made my heart start battering against my ribcage, as if it wanted to get out and flutter round Freddie's head like a cartoon bluebird.

And whatever Kayla said, I couldn't help feeling guilty about that.

Maybe there was a big difference between having a crush on someone and doing anything about it . . . but didn't the crush mean that you sort of wanted to?

'Need any—'

Kayla kicked me, and I abruptly coughed the squeak out of my voice.

'Need any help?' I said gruffly.

140

'Is your throat still giving you trouble?' Freddie asked. 'I'm fine – just tell me where you want these? If we're late in for training, Jez will have you running laps until lunchtime. Probably *only* you though, Dylan.'

I blinked at Freddie, surprised he'd noticed how unfair the treatment I was getting was. I made a mental note to ask him if he knew what it was all about.

Kayla pointed through the doors to one of the arrow signs. 'Just follow those. I've been using one of the offices at the back of the building. It seems like all the admin staff have a break during the holiday. And I hope you're free at lunch, because that's when we're going to enact my plan.'

As we dragged the footballs down to the office, she described the set-up she'd be using for her video. She wanted my help, and Freddie's too, which he agreed to surprisingly easily, considering what she was asking us to do sounded *insane*.

'And then I'll release the last net and let all the balls loose while I get the reaction shot,' Kayla finished.

'Both at once?' I asked.

She frowned. 'What do you mean, both at once?'

'I mean, how are you going to set off the haunted footballs *and* film what's happening at the same time? Won't it make it obvious it's a set-up if you're filming what you're doing?'

Kayla stopped still in the office doorway, her expression frozen in horror. 'You're right. I'd forgotten I was filming it too. But if I'm in the corridor, I won't have anyone to set off the traps!'

'I can do it,' came a voice from the black chair behind the office desk.

Leroy spun around and smiled at us.

Kayla's eyes went wide. 'What are you doing here?'

'Let's see,' Leroy said, looking exactly like he should have been stroking a white cat and cackling as he unveiled his evil plan. 'I noticed you kept looking in this direction when you were talking about your video last night. That unconscious body language gave me the first hint. So I tried a few of the doors down here until I found an open one, with a copy of *Rock Lobster* magazine open on the desk. It was obvious, really. And I'm here to check none of those are Feet of the Future balls.'

He stood up and paced over to the netting. Freddie raised an eyebrow as Leroy made his inspection. The balls were all made of plastic, and some of them had *Congratulations!* written on them in glitter glue (Kayla didn't think that would show up on film). Leroy still took the time to look at every single one.

'Well?' Kayla growled, after what felt like an hour. 'Do we pass, or are you turning me into the football fuzz?'

Leroy straightened up, leaving the kind of silence

game-show presenters do when they're about to tell somebody they've just lost their prize money.

'They're fine,' he said, finally. 'And I'll help you with the video if you like. I have some performing experience: I played 'young' St David in a *Visit Wales* video when I was five.'

Kayla's face was still stony. I stepped in before she snapped hard enough to break him.

'That would be great, Leroy. But no acting required – we just need you to drop some balls,' I said.

'If that's all sorted, has anybody noticed we're running late?' Freddie said from the doorway.

I looked at the clock. Two minutes past nine.

At five past, me, Freddie and Leroy burst on to the training centre's indoor pitch. If nothing else, all the laps had really been good for building up my speed.

Chidi had been given the job of taking the register, and by some actual miracle, he hadn't even started yet, too busy doing a comedy routine for the rest of the team. He shot a wink at us as we ran across to line up with the rest.

'Here we go, then: Frederick Alton.'

'Yes, Chid,' Freddie called out, slipping into his spot at the front of the line, not quite too out of breath to laugh.

'Alton – heir to the Towers, right, Fred? Life a roller coaster with you, is it?'

'I'd say it's fun *and* fair,' Freddie answered, holding out his hand for a high five.

God, he was *so* cool. One day, it was going to stop being amazing that we were somehow becoming friends, but today definitely wasn't it.

Chidi went on through the names in the lower part of the register, until he got to 'Dylan Ker—'

'Dylan Kershaw was *late*,' a voice cut in.

It was Laurie Deering, Jez's occasional assistant, now becoming a pretty constant bane of my life. Right on cue, Jez strolled out on to the pitch.

'Why doesn't that surprise me? I'd have you running laps again, Kershaw, but I'm naming squad positions later, and right now the only position I know you're good for is running for the tea.'

He laughed, a deep grunt, with Laurie's high-pitched giggle raised over the top. Laurie was my biggest competition for centre forward, the position I knew I played best in. I could still pull off some good moves in the midfield or on the wing, but I was a natural scorer. It made sense to put me as close as possible to the goal.

Jez took a sip from the cup of coffee he'd brought out with him, *#1 COACH* emblazoned on the front. 'Anyway, we'd better let you have some play this morning, or I'll get your mummy whining to me about how it's not fair. We'll stick you in front of the goal.'

I breathed a sigh of relief. This was perfect – now I could really start to show what I was capable of.

And then Jez tossed me a pair of goalkeeper gloves and smiled.

TWENTY-TWO

Keeper really, *really* wasn't my position.

I made a great striker. Before I'd left the school team, I'd been their number one, with the most goals scored in any local school season in history.

I wasn't too bad in most other positions, either. I was quick on my feet, and if I got down the pitch fast enough, sometimes I could even break out from a position at the back and get the ball to our end. It wasn't too much of a boast to say I was good with my feet.

My hands, though? I was *useless* with those.

Laurie had spent the whole practice match aiming the ball directly at my head, and I had to admit, he didn't exactly have terrible aim. As I stood praying for the full-time whistle to blow, I rubbed my cheek and wondered how long it would take for my face to turn as black and blue as it felt.

The worst part was, I hadn't managed to stop any goals. Even the shots that hit me somehow rolled right off my nose into the corner of the net. Jez had split us into two teams and mine was 8–0 down. It didn't even matter that one of those was an own goal (Leroy had jumped the wrong way into a header), I was still the one who let it in.

Still, at least I was getting to watch Freddie play. He was a total natural. It didn't seem to matter where on the pitch he was, the game suddenly started revolving around him. He was a certain bet to be made captain after this.

And he was heading my way.

As the winger for the opposing team, so far Freddie had been responsible for getting the ball into a clear part of the pitch before opening up a chance for Laurie to shoot. But as I scanned the pitch in a panic, I could see Laurie and Chidi had collided with each other and were now trying to get untangled from a knot of limbs.

Azi had found some space just ahead of the goal, and I silently prayed for Freddie to pass it to him, but we both knew Azi kicked like he was wearing two left boots with their laces tied together.

Freddie looked up at me, his blue eyes set on mine, and I knew he was going to have a go at goal.

I centred myself.

I bent my knees the slightest bit, keeping my feet loose, ready to spring up or crouch down if I had to.

I watched Freddie like a hawk, looking for any slip of body language that might tell me which way he was going to go. His gaze flicked up to the left side of the bar.

Left. He was going to go left. I was going to save the last ball of the match and redeem myself (almost) totally in front of Jez and the rest of the camp.

Freddie's toe flicked the ball. It went left. I went left. My hand stretched out to the side, bulky glove ready to break the impact of the ball and send it bouncing harmlessly back out of the goal. It made contact. I had it. I had it.

I had somehow flicked it straight back into my own face.

My yell of victory became a yelp of pain as I took yet another blow to the nose, but I could still save this. The ball dropped down. I scrabbled to catch it, but somehow, impossibly, it slipped through my hands.

My head dipped to see where it was going, just as it bounced up and straight into my face again.

I could hear someone laughing on the terraces.

It only got louder as the ball bounced one more time, then, as I was clasping a protective hand over my nose, rolled between my legs and into the goal.

The final whistle blew: 9–0.

Somehow, I didn't think I'd make man of the match for this one.

'Sorry.' Freddie winced as he jogged up to me, checking to see what kind of mincemeat I'd made of my own face. 'I didn't mean for you to—'

148

'Completely humiliate myself?' I asked. 'It's not your fault. Apparently I'm just really, really good at it.'

'Goalie's just not your position, is it,' Freddie said. 'I was trying to feed you an easy one, that's all.'

He was taking pity on me, and I still messed it up. Just when I thought I'd dug the deepest humiliation pit possible, it turned out there was a trapdoor of shame to fall through underneath.

'LUNCH,' Jez yelled from the centre line. 'You can go and nurse your wounds, Kershaw. Just get back on time, yeah? Anyone not here when I hand out team places doesn't get one.'

I wasn't even sure I wanted to know any more. He'd probably put me in goal just so I could be laughed at by an entire crowd of strangers. I trailed miserably off the pitch, trying to ignore the variety of sympathetic or mocking looks I was getting from the rest of the team.

'Sandwich for lunch, Kershaw?' Chidi asked, as I walked past him. 'Need someone to hold it for you?' He mimed taking a big bite of something invisible that immediately fell out of his hands, then he dropped and rolled on the ground, flailing about as he tried (and failed) to catch it. His talents were wasted on football, really.

I stalked off into the changing room while he was busy wiping invisible egg mayo from his shirt.

Leroy caught up with me. 'Bad luck out there. I don't know about you, but my game always improves under pressure. Maybe you'll play better on the big day?'

'Maybe I'd play better in literally *any* other position on the pitch,' I replied, trying not to meet his eyes. Leroy was probably the weakest player in the group, and it felt more embarrassing than comforting to be getting sympathy from him. If I hadn't been such a disaster between the goalposts, Leroy's own goal would have been what everyone was laughing at.

Maybe it was unfair to wish that had happened, but I couldn't help it. Football was the *one thing* I was really good at. Being put in a position where I wasn't allowed to prove that felt like having something stolen from me.

Maybe Dad was right when he talked about football being in my blood, after all. I definitely felt like I'd taken an injury worse than a few bruises round my nose.

My pride was stinging just as badly.

'OK.' I turned round to face Leroy once we were alone in the changing room. 'So we just need to find Kayla, make sure she's got everything set up, and then wait for Freddie to—'

'No time to *wait* for anything!' Freddie burst through the doors, Kayla behind him looking unusually flustered. 'She's early! Lacey Laine is already on her way!'

TWENTY-THREE

There was no opportunity to ask questions. We all sprang into action. Freddie bounded back down the hall the way he'd come to catch Lacey on her way to make her daily delivery of Jez Dutton's fancy artisan lunch – and to somehow talk her into taking a scenic route down one of the training centre's back halls.

Mc, Kayla and Leroy had to get ready to give her the shock of her life.

Kayla's whole plan for making her video go viral was to use the celebrity factor. She was going to make Lacey Laine think she was trapped in a haunted hallway (thanks to some 'special effects' operated by us) and catch her reaction on camera. Even if the final result wasn't as spooky as some of the other entries, if even a tiny fraction of Lacey's three million social media followers decided to watch it, she'd crush the competition easily.

We just had to make sure this worked.

There wasn't much time to listen to Kayla's instructions about timing or coordination. It seemed like it would be easy enough – most of the effects were operated by tugging on a rope or pushing something over. With Lacey's high heels clicking down the hall towards us, we were just going to have to trust to fate.

'Break a leg!' Leroy whispered to me, as he wedged himself behind the set of lockers I was clambering on top of. I was still a bit worried he had ambitions to take the starring role. Maybe that pre-school *Visit Wales* video had gone to his head.

I didn't have a chance to check. I dragged myself along the tops of the lockers on my stomach. At the other end of the hall, Kayla was shutting herself inside one, ready to film through the gaps.

'I'm sorry, Miss Laine – it looks like there's nothing down here after all,' Freddie was saying.

'Oh, call me Lacey – everybody does. I've been thinking about dropping the last name, anyway. It's more unique. You don't meet a lot of Lacies, do you?'

I peered over the top of the lockers to get a look at her outfit: a fluffy yellow puffball skirt and top with yellow feathers in her hair – it was like she was dressing up as a different character from *Sesame Street* every day.

Freddie cleared his throat. When he spoke again, I noticed his voice had gone a little . . . squeaky. Almost muppet-like. 'No. No, you don't.'

'But you say people have heard noises down this hall?'

'That's right. One of the lads said it was almost

like crying. We thought a stray cat might have got in somewhere, and I read in CLASSY magazine that you're an animal lover . . .'

Freddie Alton reads CLASSY magazine? I'd seen it in the newsagents. It was mostly soap operas and real-life stories with titles like 'Possessed by Princess Diana' and 'Help! My Dog's Addicted to Online Dating!'

I was almost too distracted to hear Freddie giving me my cue: 'Maybe if we're quiet for a minute, we'll hear something.'

I scrabbled to type Kayla's number into my phone. Last night, she'd changed her ringtone to the sound of a ghostly child we'd recorded from one of the horror movies on TV. As I hit the call button, the sound started echoing out of the locker she was hiding in.

Below me, I watched Lacey tilt her head. 'I do hear something. But I don't think that's a cat . . .'

Next, it was Leroy's turn. He shook the locker he was hiding behind until the door slowly creaked open by itself. Inside, Kayla had decorated the locker with candles, flowers, and a black and white photo of one of the current England Under-21s squad I'd happened to have tucked into the pocket of my kitbag. I'd been carrying it round with me for ages, so it looked tattered and worn. (He had really amazing arms, and he could pull off the best double lunge I'd ever seen. For some reason, Kayla didn't believe me when I told her I carried the picture for luck.)

'Isn't that . . . Marcello Marquisa?' Freddie said, managing to sound a little bit surprised.

'Who?' Lacey asked.

'Oh, he was a star player once. Tipped for glory. But that was before the . . . accident.'

Freddie was playing his part well. Leaning over the top of the lockers for a better look, I could see Lacey wrap her arms tight round herself, as though there were a chill in the air.

This might actually be working.

'The accident?'

'They say it happened back here, actually. No one knows the whole story, only that Marcello was carried out in a sheet soaked in blood and—'

'And?' Lacey was leaning in towards Freddie now, their heads almost touching.

I felt a small, strange twist of jealousy.

'And he was *never seen again.*'

There was silence.

Freddie cleared his throat. '*Never, ever again.*'

Wait, that was another cue! Snapping out of the spell Freddie's voice had put on me, I slowly rolled the first football off the locker next to me. Lacey jumped as it hit the floor next to her and bounced down the hall.

Behind the lockers, Leroy ran his nails down the metal, making a screeching, scrabbling noise. Then he tugged the knot free on the rope that held up a banner along the hallway. It folded and fell to the floor at Lacey's feet, the words *IMPROVE YOUR SKILL TODAY* becoming simply *KILL TODAY*.

Lacey yelped.

I rolled another football off the tops of the lockers. Then another. And another. Soon, the hallway was filled with Freddie's mum's faintly glittery footballs, creating chaos. Now I just had to release the goal net Kayla had strung up over the hallway, and the plan would have gone off flawlessly.

Except, Leroy was really getting into his role, rattling the lockers as if they were all full of ghostly footballers trying to scratch and shake their way out. He'd moved along from the one he was stationed behind and was shaking the one next to me. It kept almost making me lose my balance as I reached up to grab the end of the net.

'*Stop it*,' I hissed back at him, hoping my voice would be covered by Kayla's crying child. 'Stop it – I'm going to fall.'

Leroy didn't hear me. I don't think he even knew which locker I was balancing on. He stepped behind my locker and gave it a shove, tipping it forward.

Tipping me, standing right on the edge, forward.

I grabbed the goal net and yelled 'GET OUT OF THE WAY' as the locker went down.

Lacey looked up for one – brief – moment, then grabbed Freddie and made a dive to the left that would have saved any goal in history.

The locker fell forward, bouncing safely and almost silently on the raft of novelty footballs that filled the hall, and I came down after it, wrapped in the goal net, breaking my fall on something soft and warm and . . . blond and swearing quite loudly.

Slowly, I unwrapped my arms from Freddie Alton's waist.

'Sorry, I'm sorry! I didn't mean to. I was trying to land on . . .' Anything – literally anything else. I took a deep breath, trying not to give in to panic. 'My face?'

He groaned. 'Well, I'm glad you didn't manage that. But could you get up, please? Your leg's wedged somewhere really uncomfortable.'

I was already *trying* to stand up, obviously. I'd just clotheslined the best-looking boy in my school, probably in my *town*, right when we were starting to become sort of friends. Of course I was trying to get up.

'I will. I definitely will. It's just.'

There was something stopping me. Well, us.

In the flailing moment of panic as I landed, I'd got Freddie and me completely tied up in the net.

TWENTY-FOUR

'So you're trying to make a movie?' Lacey Laine asked, looking up at Kayla. She was sitting on my legs because I was finding it too difficult not to squirm while she cut me and Freddie out of the goal net using her pastel-pink nail scissors.

'A viral video,' Kayla told her. She'd pulled up a chair and was observing the rescue process at the same time as scrolling through the footage on her phone and directing Leroy on where to put all the mess he was clearing up. 'They have to be short and exciting – they're for people with no attention spans who can't follow a plot.'

'Like cats playing the piano,' Leroy said, folding the KILL TODAY banner up and hauling it into the office.

'Or a job interview,' Freddie added, 'where the window's actually an HDTV screen showing footage of the world ending right outside – ooof – thank you.' Freddie was finally free enough to move the lower part of his body out of such close contact with my knee.

'Or people eating every single item on a fast-food menu. Or demonstrating how to wrap gifts.' I tried to think of the strangest videos I'd seen.

157

'I watch those! *Sooo* soothing.' Lacey clapped her hands. 'But what I don't understand is why you didn't just *ask* me to be in it.'

'Because we wanted it to be spontaneous,' Kayla said.

'And you're really famous,' put in Leroy, arms full of footballs.

'Basically,' I said, 'we just assumed you'd say no.'

Lacey nodded, snipping the last of the netting loose so that Freddie could finally roll out of my arms. I tried to look just as relieved as him when he did.

'So you're trying to win the chance to meet this band you really like –' Lacey nodded at Kayla – 'who you could probably meet anyway, because they're, like, staying right down your hall, but you want to win this contest and meet them as a fellow creative?'

'An *auteur*,' Kayla agreed, obviously delighted by being so understood. 'It means the same as creator, but only creative people know that,' she added for my – uncreative – benefit.

'And this video you're making could end up being seen by thousands of people, which would be super good for my profile,' Lacey finished. She scratched her chin with one glittery manicured nail. 'So . . . OK.'

'OK?' I asked, shaking my head. 'You want to help us? We almost dropped a locker on you.'

'Right, so about that part,' Lacey said.

Kayla leaned in, nodding furiously.

'I'll star in your video, but we're going to have to reshoot the end.'

In the office, Leroy let out a long, tortured groan, and started dragging the banners and balls back the way he'd come.

Surprising everyone, Lacey Laine turned out to be a pretty good actress. The second time around, she let out a shriek that made the hairs on my arms stand on end when the balls started filling the hallway around her, and we kept in the part where she heroically shoved Freddie out of the way. She even helped us (or mostly Leroy) tidy up again when it was all done, before giving Kayla her email so she could send her a copy of the final edit, retrieving the bag she'd brought with Jez's lunch and heading briskly off towards the indoor pitch.

Freddie and I followed not long after, since Leroy and Kayla had gotten into another argument about whether he should be credited as 'assistant director' or 'director's assistant', and I already had enough of a headache from taking nine goals to the face, followed by falling off a locker.

Though I almost managed to add to it by slipping on a copy of MOXY Magazine as we wandered back towards the changing room. We'd missed most of lunch, but I was too worried about Jez assigning team positions to feel hungry. If I got stuck in a defensive spot somewhere in the back, I knew Dad would think I'd messed up somewhere. They weren't bad positions; they just weren't where I played my best.

'Isn't this Lacey's?' I said, picking up the magazine. It was much heavier than I'd expected. I hadn't realized fashion and gossip were such weighty subjects.

'Maybe she's finished with it?' Freddie suggested.

'Maybe . . .' I flipped through a few pages and tucked it under my arm. 'I'll give it back to her later anyway, just in case. I feel like I owe her one . . . or, you know, one million, after today. Helping us out with the video, I mean.'

'And helping us out of a human reef knot?' Freddie raised his eyebrows.

I'd thought I was doing well keeping my voice at a level audible to humans instead of dogs, but it squeaked upwards in reply. 'That too.'

'Well –' Freddie shrugged – 'once your foot wasn't cutting off my circulation, it wasn't so bad. By which I mean, if you wanted to do it again without the film crew, you could always let me know.'

He shouldered his bag and swung the changing-room doors open, letting out a rush of noise from inside.

I didn't move. Just watched the door swing inevitably

towards my poor, long-suffering nose. Just then, I didn't think I'd even feel it.

But a hand reached out and stopped the door before it could hit me. Freddie leaned back through, eyebrows raised. 'Are you coming or not?'

Legs. If I concentrated really hard, I *knew* I could remember how to use my legs.

'Um.' I took a deep breath and a wobbly step forward. 'Yeah.'

The room fell quiet as I walked in, and for a moment, I thought it was because of me. The whole team were crowded on to the benches or hanging off the clothes rails. Maybe they were shocked I'd bothered to come back after the morning's humiliation. Maybe my bruised nose had blown up to the size of a blimp, and nobody had told me.

Subtly, I tried crossing my eyes to check it out. It still looked normal size. It hadn't even changed colour from its usual pink.

Maybe Kayla's video footage had accidentally been beamed on to all their phones, and they'd just been watching me trying not to look like I was at all happy about being tangled up with Freddie.

Or maybe it was just that Jez Dutton had walked in right behind me, with Leroy and Laurie Deering standing to either side.

161

'Right then.' He sniffed and rubbed his nose dry on one sleeve of his shirt, before flapping an A4 sheet of paper out in front of him. 'I hope you lot appreciate me spending my whole lunchtime slaving over this. Positions for the end-of-week match. First, and most important, central midfield, and your captain from now till then.'

Freddie sat down hard on the end of one of the benches. Jez didn't even look over at him.

'Now, I may not look it, but I'm a benevolent man. I believe in second chances. Giving people the chance to prove themselves. And a good captain's someone who knows they need to prove themselves, not some show pony who finds it easy.'

Second chances? Prove themselves? I stared hard at the ground. There was no way Jez would give me the captain's role over Freddie, surely. Everyone knew he deserved that.

Jez tilted his head to look at Leroy. 'You said you perform best under pressure, yeah?'

Leroy nodded, looking anxious.

'Great,' Jez said. 'You're captain. Laurie Deering, you'll be centre forward. Azi and Josh, you're in back. Chidi, you'll be sweeper . . .'

He went on. It was a list that left almost everyone looking at each other in confusion over what they'd been selected for, but nobody more than me. Because Jez had read out every single position, right through to Aaron Addington in goal, and I wasn't any of them.

As if he could read my mind, he fixed his steely eyes on me. 'And Kershaw, you're in reserve. You can watch the match from the subs bench, but I wouldn't get too excited – you won't be playing.'

He crunched up the sheet of paper and chucked it into the room.

'Frankly, I'm already letting you closer to the pitch than you deserve.'

TWENTY-FIVE

I was a substitute. Not even a starting player. That meant that if no one else got injured, or needed a break, I'd end up spending the entire end-of-week match watching from the bench.

Dad had made a banner to wave just for me, and he might as well have been coming to watch me sit in the park.

I'd spent the whole afternoon in a sort of daze, getting hot flushes whenever I thought about Freddie's arms wrapped round me, and cold shivers when my brain dragged itself back to picturing Dad's face when I had to tell him about the match.

At least, by the end of a long afternoon feeling like I'd got caught in a doorway between the North Pole and the Sahara, I'd come up with a solution to *one* of my problems.

I just wasn't going to tell Dad. Or Mum. At all.

Something was bound to happen before the match to mean I wouldn't have to. Somebody would call in with flu, or break something painful but non-essential, and I'd be ready to step up. Or maybe this was just Jez trying to scare me, and tomorrow it would turn out to be a double bluff.

There was still time. In two days, someone else might annoy him even more than I somehow had, and he'd switch our roles.

It was all going to work out, so there was no *point* telling anyone about it before I absolutely had to. Dad would only come down and create a fuss, and then I'd die of embarrassment, and Jez would probably *still* prop me up on the bench for everyone to laugh at, even as rigor mortis gradually set in.

I wasn't even going to tell Kayla. That felt wrong, somehow, but I knew how angry she'd be on my behalf, and my parents were bound to figure out something was up if she started walking round like a bull in search of a matador to gore.

Although, that was ignoring her weird psychic ability to figure out when something was wrong with me . . . She knew as soon as I got in the car. We were all going to a restaurant for an evening hopefully uninterrupted by hamsters that go bump in the night. I'd been looking forward to it all day. But now I was dreading having to spend a family meal living a lie.

Kayla needled me in the ribs with an elbow as soon as Dad turned up the radio too loud for him to overhear what we were saying.

'What's the matter?'

See? I looked at Kayla, open-mouthed. 'How did you know something *was*?'

'You look like someone gave your puppy to a farm, then told you it got run over by a car, Dylan. You look miserable. That was my first clue.'

She really was uncanny.

I still couldn't tell her about Jez singling me out, though. She'd be snorting fury over her steak and chips. So I went for the slightly less awful option.

'You know how I've been feeling weird about my crush on Freddie?'

Kayla nodded.

'Well, the part I didn't say was . . . the part that makes it difficult is . . .'

Is it would be fine if it was *just* a crush. If he was just a bit distracting, but nothing would ever – *could* ever happen. That wasn't the problem. The problem was . . .

'The part that makes it difficult is that I think he has a crush on me too.'

Kayla's eyes widened. I knew it was bad, but I hadn't expected her to look quite so shocked. She'd had a new boyfriend every term last year at school, plus Summer over the summer, so usually she took matters of romance in her stride. Not this, though. She clutched my arm.

'Oh, no.'

I nodded sadly. 'Oh, yes.'

'Oh, Dylan.'

She looked so concerned, I was starting to wonder if I hadn't been worried *enough*. I paused while the presenter on the radio ran though his spiel between songs, looking over my shoulder to check my little brother wasn't listening in from his window seat. Once another 'ultimate 80s classic' started rattling the windows, I asked, 'What? What is it?'

Kayla bit her lip. 'It's just . . . I'd been hoping you wouldn't *notice*.'

She'd what? I blinked at her. 'You'd what?'

'At least until the week was over. You're usually so oblivious to obvious things like this.'

'I don't . . . Excuse me?'

'I mean, you seem to think it's so impossible anyone might like you. They usually have to put on a tutu and perform their intentions to you by way of interpretive dance before you become even vaguely aware of it. Come to think of it, isn't that almost exactly what Leo did?'

'What?' I was baffled by this sudden turn of events. '*No*. I suppose . . . I did see him dancing, and that was when I realized . . . Look, that isn't important. We're talking about Freddie Alton now. You know, Freddie Alton, sports captain at school? Perfect in every way?

So good-looking even Lacey Laine was willing to follow him into a haunted hallway looking for an imaginary cat?' I folded my arms. 'Why would I ever think someone like that would like someone like me?'

Kayla ticked off a silent checklist on her fingers. 'Oh, I can think of a few reasons. So why do you think it now?'

'Because he told me,' I said huffily.

'Ah.' Kayla sighed and relaxed back in her seat. 'Well, that explains it. Panic over. You haven't developed sudden powers of observation at all. Only powers of hearing, and you had those before.'

Somehow this all seemed very unfair on me. Kayla clicked her tongue.

'I did hope you wouldn't figure it out while you were still playing together, though.'

She was *so* confusing. 'Why?'

'Because you're going to find some way to torture yourself about it. I know you,' she said. 'It's just what you do.'

'I do *not*,' I hissed, and I slumped back, staring through the car window.

A second later, I turned back to her. 'But what am I supposed to *do*? I'm still getting used to one person I like liking me. How am I supposed to cope with two?'

'Three,' Kayla said.

I frowned at her, and she pointed at herself.

'Always nice to be completely overlooked by you, Dylan. I happen to like you too. Not *that* way, but it shouldn't be so impossible that other people might.'

'You know what I mean, though. *That way* makes things different. It would be much easier if it was just you.'

She laughed. 'Well, maybe I should try growing a couple of feet and a beard . . . and you can date me instead. I'm much less complicated.'

'Except you like girls now,' I reminded her.

'No – I like boys *and* girls,' she corrected. 'It's called being bi.'

I knew that, obviously. 'I've been meaning to ask, actually. You know there's supposed to be an instinctive way gay people figure out who else is like them?'

'Gaydar?' Kayla tried.

I nodded. 'Yeah. Well how do *bi* people do it?'

Kayla smiled and raised her eyebrows mysteriously. 'Dylan, I can't believe you've never heard of bi-noculars.'

Any response I wanted to give to that got cut off as Dad pulled the car into a space on the side of the street, dousing the version of 'Eternal Flame' that Mum had been singing along to. He rapped on the window.

'This looks like the place.'

I wasn't sure which restaurant he meant, but the street up ahead was hung with bunting, like someone was having a party. The whole place was decked with all the colours of the rainbow.

Kayla opened the door on her side, and we both piled out to see what Dad had been pointing at. On the wall opposite us, someone had painted a mural. An oversized street sign, marked with the words *OUR GAY VILLAGE*.

Dad was grinning. 'I just thought it might be something you'd like to see.'

TWENTY-SIX

It turned out a gay village wasn't just a rural community full of very happy people. Manchester's gay village was based around a street right in the centre of the city, running alongside a canal. Dad said it was just somewhere most people *weren't* straight, rather than the other way around, but as we looked through the windows of the bars and restaurants, and watched people walking by, I couldn't help thinking it was a bit more than that.

It was a place where it didn't feel *different* not to be straight. Or at least, not like being different might be a bad thing.

It's stupid, really, feeling bad about being different, because the only thing most people have in common is that we're all a bit different somehow. We're all a unique combination of differences: like how some people are tall, and some are short, and some people like runny cheese, and some people would rather bathe in the distilled essence of human feet than put a stinky brie near their mouths. It's our own assortment of different bits that makes us who we are.

But in the gay village, on Canal Street, men could hold hands with men, and women could hold hands with women, and no one would look at them like it was an unusual thing to do. They wouldn't have to worry about getting a comment from someone who didn't understand how other people could be different to them.

And I thought that must be why the people who came here called it a village, not just a street. Because a village is a kind of community, really, and this felt a little bit like that.

Just ahead of me, Jude was loudly singing a rainbow, while Mum and Dad reminded him which order the colours went.

Kayla hooked her elbow round mine and leaned her head against my shoulder. 'What are you thinking?'

'Just that I really, really wish I could come here with Leo one day,' I said. 'No offence or anything. I like being here with you too. It's just not—'

'*The same*,' Kayla finished. 'But it's Leo you're thinking about?'

I closed my eyes for a minute and pictured myself holding his hand. No one else came to mind, even for a moment. Not even Tom Holland and his Spider-Man arms. 'Yeah.'

'Then I don't think you need to worry about Freddie's crush.'

I sighed. 'But what if things don't work out? What if Leo came here and thought about holding hands with some gorgeous dancer instead? Someone who can kick their ankle up by their head and lift another person up like they're making them fly? What if Leo's already going off me, and by the time I find out, Freddie's had time to stop liking me too? And what if I end up alone and lonely, photoshopping myself into holiday brochure pictures and posting them on social media to make it look like I have a life?'

Kayla nudged a pebble with her foot and watched it rattle down into the canal. 'Well. I suppose that's possible, in a world where I stop existing for no apparent reason, and Leo and Freddie are the only two people to find you tolerable for the rest of your life.'

'See?' I said. 'It's possible! If I wait for the chance to hold hands with Leo somewhere like this, that could be how things end up.'

'Or,' Kayla countered, 'if you wait for the chance to hold hands with Leo somewhere like this, it could happen, and be the best day of your life.'

'So what do I do?' I asked desperately.

'Well, Dylan,' she said. 'I suppose you decide whether it's worth waiting to find out which way things go.'

'Hurry up! We're getting tiny sandwiches!' Jude yelled across from the doorway of a tea room.

Mum was leaning on the back of his chair, reading the menu for herself despite Jude's proclamation. And Dad was watching me watching everything else, with the kind of smile on his face that made me forgive him for dragging me to football camp when I'd wanted to sit at home and mope. It even made me forgive him for most of the terrible football chants he came up with.

And it made me want to make him proud, even more than ever.

Something *had* to get me off that subs bench before the game.

Dad spent most of the meal finding new ways to ask how things at Feet of the Future were going, while I spent most of it finding new ways of dodging the question.

By the time we were heading back to the hotel, I had a trickle of cold sweat running down the back of my neck, and I'd somehow managed to convince Dad that Jez wasn't telling anyone which positions they'd be playing until the morning of the match because he liked keeping people on their toes.

It wasn't really a lie. I definitely intended to find out I had a new position before the match, and Jez kept me on my toes all the time, running his ridiculous laps.

Luckily Jude was happy to take all the attention I was trying to avoid. He showed Dad some of the new moves he was learning in the hotel car park, swerving his powerchair between the cars like they were part of a slalom course. I might have been a gigantic disappointment waiting to happen, but maybe Jude was going to be the real athlete in the family.

Or, like Dad, maybe I was getting ahead of myself just a bit. I definitely reassessed my opinion once he ran over my toes. 'Hey, watch where you're going, or I'll report you for drunk driving.'

'He only had a milkshake!' Kayla laughed.

'He had two,' I reminded her. 'That's the problem – he's drunk on sugar.'

But Jude was swerving off in another direction now.

Mum reached out to put a steadying hand on the back of his chair. 'And where do you think you're going?'

Jude tipped his head back to look up at her. 'I want to see how many hamsters they've got in that van!'

A vanload of hamsters sounded like it was asking for trouble, considering the problems we were having with just one. I looked up to see what he meant. There was a white van parked outside the hotel.

'That's not a hamster on the side of the van – that's a rat,' I corrected him. 'And it doesn't say *hamster* on it, either. What does it say?'

Jude frowned hard and tried spelling out the world phonetically. 'Puh – es – tuh. Pest?'

'It says *Pest Control*,' Kayla said, her voice low and serious. 'And it looks like they're heading inside our hotel.'

TWENTY-SEVEN

Jude might have been too young and full of milkshake to fully appreciate the gravity of the situation, but the feeling of dread that settled in my chest on seeing the pest-control van only grew as we passed the few stray Deathsplash fans dedicated enough to lurk outside the hotel all night and made our way into the lobby.

Four men in beige boiler suits were listening intently while Alfie told them all about the 'rat' he'd seen in our corridor. They all wore huge backpacks capable of holding a dozen vicious traps, and as I watched, one of them was thumping a rolled-up magazine against the palm of his hand like a club.

There was no mistaking what they were here for.

This was a war on Fluffy.

Kayla and I slipped away from Mum and Dad while they went to the lifts, trying to overhear the instructions Ms Toshkhani was giving the Ratbusters.

'You will work only at night. We don't want to upset any guests when, in all probability, this is an isolated outbreak. Start with the rooms allocated to Mr and Mrs Smith – that's where the thing was last spotted.' She paused, then added grimly, 'It had crawled inside a guitar.'

Kayla let out a small, not un-ratty squeaking noise, and Ms Toshkhani looked up, her face freezing at once. Through unmoving lips, she instructed the men at twice the volume she'd been speaking before.

'Right then. It's wonderful to hear the problems in the side building are a thing of the past! We won't be needing your services again.'

'Until after midnight, when no one's around,' finished Alfie.

I was sure I saw her kick him under the counter.

'We have to find this Mr and Mrs Smith,' I whispered to Kayla. 'They've got our hamster!'

'I know who they are,' she told me through gritted teeth. 'Pretend to go to the loo and meet me outside the lifts in ten minutes. I'm going to tell your mum you're helping me with my tuck and tumble.'

I looked at her curiously.

'It's a *cheerleading move*,' she snapped. 'Now go!'

So I went. I crossed my legs and hopped a bit, trying to look as much like an innocent toilet-goer as possible, just in case Ms Toshkhani realized I was up to something . . . though once I was in the loos, it was a bit harder to hide the fact that I didn't really have anything to do.

Kayla had said ten minutes. I checked the time on my

phone, locked myself in the toilet stall, and called Leo.

It was pretty late, so I thought he must've been finished for the day and back in his room. Hopefully he wasn't so worn out by a week of intensive rehearsals that he'd fallen asleep already – it was taking him a long time to answer.

And then, when he did, it seemed like it might have been by accident. I'd started a video call, but when it connected, all I could see was the underside of his chin. The image was a little bit shaky, but Leo was laughing, and I could hear someone else in the background laughing too.

Was there someone in his room? It was too dark to see anything properly. Why was there someone in his room?

'. . . Leo?'

The scene slowly started to tilt. He was leaning sideways. Leaning against whoever he was with, while the phone slipped gradually off his lap. Then I couldn't see Leo at all, just an upwards angle of the view out of what looked like a bus window.

He wasn't rehearsing at all.

When I thought about it, I'd never actually seen him in his dance gear during any of the conversations we'd had. He never called me from rehearsals. I hadn't seen any proof that the 'something' that 'came up' to make him cancel all his plans with me really was a dance show at all. What if it was just some*one* he wanted to spend the time with more than he wanted to spend it with me?

And maybe that answered my question of whether it was worth waiting for him. I could be waiting forever while he laughed, and leaned on, and hung out with other people.

Gritting my teeth tight as something stung in the corners of my eyes, I disconnected the call, flushed the loo (for effect), and pushed open the toilet door.

It was fine. I didn't care. There were plenty of other people who liked me, if Leo had stopped.

Well, there were definitely *two* people.

Kayla. And Freddie.

Stopping by the mirror, I splashed a bit of cold water on to my face – the kind of wake-up call I needed – before going out to see if Kayla's excuse had worked.

She was waiting by the lifts, like she'd promised. Since she'd gone upstairs with my parents, she'd pulled her blue-green hair up into a tight ponytail on top of her head, changed into a different outfit (a red top and a short, bright yellow pleated skirt) and had two glittery pom-poms drooping out of her hands.

'What on earth—'

'Don't ask,' she interrupted, as the lift pinged its arrival and we entered. 'I hired it from the costume shop at home in case I needed to convince anyone I really *was* at Camp Cheer this week. And it worked. Now, I'd estimate we have about an hour to track down this hamster before your parents start expecting us back.'

'Right,' I said, trying to sound businesslike, and not like I was choking down a laugh. From the expression on her face, I wasn't sure I'd pulled it off – then again, the ponytail was pulling her face so tight that every look she gave me seemed a little bit pained. 'First things first – you said you knew who Mr and Mrs Smith were?'

'That's right,' Kayla said, pushing the lift button for our usual floor. 'It's all over the internet. Those are the decoy names celebrities use when they book into hotels. In this case . . . the Deathsplash Nightmares.'

The lift pinged again and opened into a familiar hallway, but this time Kayla didn't duck and hide behind me or rush us towards our room. She stepped out, hands on her hips.

'Are you sure?' I asked, following her as she walked over to the door we knew belonged to the band.

'Not even slightly.' Kayla glanced back over her shoulder at me. 'But we don't have a choice. We're doing this for *Fluffy*.'

She looked determined, but her hand had stopped, curled up in mid-air as if she'd grabbed on to an invisible handle. She was trembling slightly. Pop-star paralysis was striking again.

It was all up to me now.

Stepping around her, I raised a hand and knocked on the door.

It vibrated back at me. Someone was playing loud music in there, and my knock must have been lost under the bass. I tried again, first with one fist, and then with both, hammering as loudly as I could until Kayla grabbed my wrists.

'Careful, you'll have the rest of the hallway coming out to see what you want before anyone in there hears you. The weird thing is, that's not Deathsplash they're playing. The rhythm's off. I can tell by the way it vibrates under my feet. I don't think it's even *metal*.'

She elbowed me out of the way and pressed against the door, putting her ear to the wood. 'No, it's not. It's ... It's ...'

The door swung open, as the jingly beats of Abba's 'Dancing Queen' rang out into the hall. And Kayla fell forward, straight into the purple velvet arms of the Nightmare's lead singer: Rick Deathsplash.

TWENTY-EIGHT

Suddenly I was experiencing a little pop-star paralysis myself, unable to do anything except watch as Kayla fell into the arms of the man she considered the greatest artist in the history of the world . . . and then rolled back out of them again to lie in a primary-coloured pile at his feet.

Rick raised the mirrored shades he seemed to have been wearing even inside his dimly lit room and looked down at her.

'I don't touch people,' he explained in a light drawl. His voice was softer than I'd expected for someone who spent so much time screaming on his records. 'Germs . . . Alonzo?'

A man who must have been Alonzo appeared as if by magic at Rick's side, spritzed the whole of his Cadbury-purple outfit with what looked like hand sanitizer, and then vanished again. Meanwhile, Rick was watching Kayla groan and slowly pick herself up off the floor. My basic motor functions started running again just in time for me to bend down and help her up.

'Well, thank you for coming by. It really was wonderful

183

to meet you. I love the fans.' Rick had already started to vanish backwards into the room as he spoke, the door closing in his wake. 'Thank you for your support.'

'Wait!' I yelped, throwing a hand out to keep the door open a few inches – dropping Kayla again in the process. She growled and started clambering back on to her knees. 'I have something important to ask you!'

Alonzo stuck his head around the frame. 'No impromptu interviews. Rick only answers pre-approved questions.'

'It's not an interview! I just – I need to know if you've seen my little brother's hamster.'

'Nice try – very creative . . . Have a good evening.' Alonzo diligently peeled my fingers away from the edge of the door and closed it with a click.

The beat of Abba's tambourine was stifled, and the hallway went quiet again. I stuck my hand out to Kayla, but she ignored it as she staggered to her feet.

'You didn't even—'

'I know,' I said, slightly hopelessly.

'You just let him—'

'I *know.*'

She shook her head, dazed. I didn't even manage to ask if Rick had seen Fluffy; I just let him think we were crazed fans who'd somehow snuck past security. Of course, if I'd actually tried to get into the room, I think

Alonzo might have been ready to tazer me, but still. I'd failed, completely. Miserably. And Kayla . . .

'I met Rick Deathsplash . . .' she whispered to herself. 'I met his feet.'

I guessed it wasn't quite the deep connection of two creative minds she'd envisaged.

'Still,' I said sympathetically, 'at least he probably won't remember your face?'

She might have killed me then and there if someone hadn't cleared their throat from the next doorway along.

'Sorry, kids – did you say *hamster*?'

Jenna Deathsplash, vicious destroyer of drum kits, possible macrobiotic diet and chilli-topped hot-dog fan, and Kayla's ultimate heroine was beckoning us towards her room.

'It was in here,' she told us, picking up one of six black and gold guitars lined up against the wall. They played electric ones onstage, but these were the retro wooden kind that smashed more impressively in their big numbers. 'I wouldn't have snitched, but Antoni's got a phobia. Said he couldn't sleep for imagining tiny little feet pitter-pattering about. Then all of a sudden, everyone's talking about calling in the exterminators, so I found the poor little creature the only route out of here I could.'

Warily I eyed the curtains flapping in the cool night breeze. 'Not the window?'

'No, no,' Jenna reassured quickly. 'The housekeeping service. I popped him in their basket of miniature shampoos when no one was looking and watched him get wheeled along the hall. So tell your brother I'm sorry, but his hamster must be long gone from here by now.'

'Thank you,' Kayla said, in a voice choked up with emotion that might have been Fluffy-related, but probably had more to do with standing in the same room as her long-time idol. I'd never heard her sound quite like this before. 'You deserve more recognition for humanitarian work like this.'

Jenna smiled awkwardly. 'Ah, I don't know about humanitarian. I like animals, though – I'd have felt guilty if the little guy squeaked his last on my account.'

'Hamsteritarian,' Kayla amended. 'Just as noble a cause. Without you, poor Fluffy would be scampering through the great Habitrail in the sky.'

I knew exactly what was happening to Kayla right then. I knew because it happened to me when I had to talk to someone I really, really liked. When it got so hard to find words at all that my brain just started picking ones at random and joining them together, hoping they made some kind of sense. It was like the reasonable, sensible person *usually* in charge of my brain got hijacked

186

by a toddler on a sugar high. I'd never seen it happen to anyone else before, though. I hooked my arm through Kayla's and started walking us backwards before Jenna started to think she was a complete fruit loop.

'Yeah, um, thanks for that,' I managed, trying to shove Kayla backwards through the door. 'Really. Maybe now we've got a chance of finding him before the Ratbusters do.'

'He'd be stuck on a heavenly hamster wheel . . .' Kayla was jabbering from just behind me. 'Digging through celestial sawdust . . .'

'Well, good luck with the concert and everything! Nice meeting you! Night!' Smiling through tightly gritted teeth, I pushed the door shut as I dragged Kayla out with me.

'Rolling along forever in an Elysian exercise ball, through fields of carrots as far as the eye can see, and lost – *lost to us forever!*' Kayla managed to yell out before it slammed. Then she looked at me, wild-eyed, and yelped, 'Help me! I can't stop!' and shoved a pom-pom in her mouth, biting down hard.

I pulled her down the hall with me and knocked at the door to our room. At least we knew Fluffy wouldn't be in the line of fire tonight. But if we didn't find him before the Ratbusters did, then Jude would be devastated – and we didn't have much longer to do it.

Visions of me telling my little brother that we had to go home without his hamster joined the ones I was already having of how disappointed Dad would look seeing me on the subs bench for the big match, and of Leo laughing and laughing with someone who wasn't me. Halloween wasn't for two days, but I was already being haunted.

'That's a move I haven't seen before,' Dad commented, opening the door.

Recovering herself (if not her dignity), Kayla picked pom-pom pieces out of her mouth and stalked past him. I was pretty sure she was going to scream into her pillow.

'She's got the throwing-them-in-the-air part down,' I said. 'We're still having trouble with the bit where she has to catch them with her hands.'

Dad grinned, ruffling my hair as I walked past. 'Well, we can't all be natural athletes, can we?'

He didn't know how right he was.

I checked my phone as I headed to my room – three missed calls from Leo – then silently turned it off for the night.

TWENTY-NINE

Next morning, I was ten minutes late to training, and I had twelve missed calls on my phone. There were seven unanswered texts too, and I'd turned off read receipts so Leo wouldn't even know I'd picked them up. *He* could spend the day wondering what *I* was doing, for a change. We always texted good morning to each other, though I was surprised he'd even remembered after the *great time* he'd clearly been having last night.

Well, there wasn't going to be a good-morning text from me today, or any other texts, either. I was completely, totally decided about that.

I deleted my reply to him for the twenty-third time and strolled through the changing-room doors.

I'd decided too, that being late didn't matter any more. I'd had the punishment already, so I might as well do something to deserve it. My whole life was such a disaster that Jez probably wouldn't give me a chance to play even if I showed up at 4 a.m. and scrubbed every seat in the terraces with my own toothbrush. I dumped my kitbag on one of the benches and wondered if I should bother showing my face at all.

'Kershaw? We've been waiting for you.' Jez's shadow loomed ahead of him through the door. 'Get your kit on and warm up. Alton's out injured – you're playing today.'

I was playing.

That morning, we were having a practice match against a local youth team, and I was going to take Freddie's position. I'd finally have a chance to show I wasn't just reserve material. My heart leaped into my throat, then promptly turned a spluttering somersault.

Freddie was injured?

Jogging out to warm up on the pitch, I spotted Freddie sitting on the bench where I should have been. Lacey Laine was perched next to him in a drapey white dress, looking like she'd just run out of a church in the middle of the 'Wedding March'. I headed over to them, eyeing the youth team doing their own warm-ups on the other side of the pitch.

'You can't be hurt – the match is tomorrow!' I burst out as soon as I saw Freddie. 'Your mum—'

'Won't know anything about it – don't worry,' Freddie said, flapping his hands out to cool me down. 'I just told Jez I'd got a toe sprain so he'd give you a go in a spot where you can get some actual play. Once he sees what you can do, he's bound to let you on tomorrow – even if it's not in my place.'

I didn't know what to say. Freddie was running the risk of getting stepped down or moved to a worse position for tomorrow, all so I'd have my chance. It might have been the nicest thing anyone had ever done for me (if I didn't count Leo once giving me an umbrella to protect me from an emotional rain cloud, and Kayla staying my best friend even when I'd been a pretty bad friend to her, sometimes). I could have kissed him for it.

'You're really not hurt?' I asked.

'Stubbed my toe on one of the benches. I was hopping about when Jez came in this morning. That's what gave me the idea.' He looked really pleased with himself. 'Anyway, I was telling Lacey that I wouldn't really mind if I *didn't* play tomorrow.'

I looked across at Lacey in surprise.

She waved and blew me a little kiss. 'Freddie's got all sorts of talents – we have that in common.'

A little blush started to creep up Freddie's neck. 'I don't know about that. But football's not *really* what I want to do. Actually, I want to be a doctor more than anything, but I don't know how to tell my mum. She'll be so disappointed.'

Weirdly, this week was starting to make me realize that football really *was* something I wanted to stay involved in. Not just because it made Dad happy, but because I loved it too. Way more than I'd realized.

For now, I was just really, really grateful that Freddie was willing to help me.

'I know Mum thinks I have a chance of making it big,' he was saying. 'But I just love science so much.'

That reminded me. 'Speaking of science. Lacey, I think I've got something of yours.'

I dug around in my bag and handed over her copy of *MOXY*. I'd had a look at it that morning because I was bored, and totally not because I wanted to look at an article titled 'Twelve Surprising Ways to Keep Your Man'. Number one was 'Don't moan when he's watching sports. Go out with the girls and have a great time instead!' (I thought it might have been a little bit sexist.) There was more in the magazine than ways to make your boyfriend happy, though. A lot more. Like a really heavy-duty-looking textbook called *Essential Astrophysics*.

Lacey squealed as I handed the magazine back and quickly checked to make sure the book she'd hidden inside it was still there. She flashed me and Freddie a quick look at the cover.

'Well, now you know my secret too. I'm a student!' She beamed at us with a red-lipped, white-toothed megawatt smile.

'A physics student,' Freddie said, looking even more

impressed than he clearly already was. 'Are you doing a degree?'

'Oh, I've got two of those already,' Lacey said. 'I needed something a little more challenging. There's just so much *time* to fill when I'm getting manicures or blow dries. So I looked for a little something to occupy my mind.'

I'd seen the course name written inside the book. 'A *little something* like a rocket science PhD?'

Lacey clapped her hands, bracelets jingling. 'Exactly! I *told* you Freddie and I had talents in common!'

I had to hand it to her – there really was a lot more to her than met the eye.

'OI, KERSHAW!' Jez's voice echoed around the dugout. 'Are you going to exercise anything except your jaw this morning? Get over here.'

What I still couldn't really see was whatever Lacey saw in Jez.

I ran across to join him and the rest of the team in a group huddle. This was supposed to be where the manager let us know about any strategy changes and threw out some encouraging words to motivate us all to play at our absolute best.

Jez was breathing heavily as we gathered in around him. 'Right then. This team are an absolute shower – any of you lot let me down in front of them, and I'll have you strung up by your ankles. Understand? Say, "Yes, Jez."'

'. . . Yes, Jez,' we all said, after a moment of waiting for him to get to the encouraging, inspiring part.

'Well, get on with it, then.' He broke away from us and headed off the pitch without a backward glance.

I wouldn't have looked at him again, either – I thought most of us could play better without one of his pep talks – except that something caught my eye as the referee blew his whistle to start play.

It was Jez, over in one corner of the training ground. He was talking to two security guards, who were each holding one arm of a short, bright-haired girl.

THIRTY

What was Kayla doing here? The thought ran round and round in my mind as I tried to focus on the game, keeping an eye on who had possession of the ball and running into free space to be ready to take a pass if one came.

Obviously she must have been caught not attending Camp Cheer. She must have had to give them my name before they handed her over to the police for failing to be sporty in a sport-designated space. That was, unless the police were already on their way, and so were my parents, and Kayla was just waiting here until they took her away. I kept glancing over to see if I could spot the glint of handcuffs round her wrists.

This was a disaster.

I shot another quick look across. For some reason, they were letting her sit next to Lacey and Freddie in the dugout. Probably keeping her in plain sight so she couldn't make a break for it. For a moment, I pictured Kayla's life on the run: buying bottles of normal-coloured hair dye to disguise herself and dressing in monochrome. Wearing black leggings with beige cardigans. She'd never survive.

The image of bland, boring Kayla was so vivid that I almost didn't see my chance to run in for the ball. Only almost, though. I've got some kind of natural instinct when it comes to football, and even if my brain isn't completely turned on, my feet are usually already carrying me the right way. I skidded in to steal the ball . . .

And found Laurie Deering doing the exact same thing, except it didn't seem like he was aiming to take the ball – it was more like he was trying to take me out instead. He collided with me hard, sending me toppling to my knees as he turned quickly and ran for the goal.

I stayed there, stunned for a moment.

I'd just been tackled by someone from my own team.

Looking further up the pitch, I could see Leroy lying on his back, moaning. It looked like he'd been a victim of the same tactic. But before I could pick myself up, I heard the half-time whistle and a huge cheer go off at the exact same time. Laurie had scored with half a second to spare.

After checking Leroy wasn't hurt – apart from the wind that had been knocked out of him, nothing seemed out of place – I ran across to Kayla. The security guards who'd brought her in were standing off to one side, their arms folded.

I dashed up to her. 'Don't worry – I'll bust you out!' I whispered.

She frowned at me. 'Sorry – you'll what?'

'Out of prison!' I breathed. 'I'll smuggle in a nail file or a bar of soap or something. You won't have to rot away for long.'

'I think it's supposed to be a nail file *in* a bar of soap,' Kayla said slowly. 'I don't know how anyone would escape using soap alone, unless they tried to slip between the bars. And I don't even think prisons *have* many bars any more, so the nail file wouldn't be much good, either. But, Dylan, you don't have to—'

'What's going on here?' one of the guards said, wandering over.

I'd just have to take full responsibility. I'd say Kayla was my lucky charm. I couldn't play without her, so I'd smuggled her in. Some people kept Troll Dolls with them for luck; I just had my own small, colourful-haired accessory.

I looked up at the guard. 'She's with—'

'Me,' Lacey Laine cut in. 'I don't think I've introduced my new personal assistant yet, have I? Meet Kayla Flores.'

Kayla shot me a winning smile.

'These boys were just sticking around to watch the match. Weren't you, fellas?'

From the expression on the guard's face, it looked more like he was sticking around to watch Lacey Laine, but I wasn't going to argue. Just so long as Kayla didn't have a future behind bars.

Jez appeared behind me, clamping a hand down on my shoulder. 'Chat up my girlfriend every chance you get, don't you, Kershaw? But the thing you should know is, she doesn't like seafood.'

I must have looked as baffled as I felt, because he smiled, showing every tooth in his mouth. 'She's not into shrimp. Especially not little shrimps like you who can't even stay on their feet till half-time. You're showing me up – and you don't want to show me up, do you?'

I didn't want to show Jez up, *or* chat up his girlfriend, but it felt like he was constantly putting my intentions through a translation programme and coming out with something I didn't mean.

It was easier to just give him the answer he wanted. 'No, Jez.'

'Then get back out there and get lucky, cos you ain't getting lucky anywhere else.'

At least that part was sort of true – luck really hadn't been on my side recently. At least when it came to Feet of the Future, I still had a chance to turn things around. For the second half of the match, I was going to play my socks off.

Not literally, obviously. If you're going to wear brand-new football boots without socks, you might as well just strap a cheese grater to the back of each foot, because that's what it feels like. No, I definitely had the appropriate footwear. I was just going to be brilliant.

And I was. The thing with football is that no star player gets to be that way without helping the rest of the team. Sometimes the best player in the squad is the one setting up for other people to score. Sure, they don't get the goals and the glory – they don't get to make up a little dance to do on the sidelines while people run up to high-five them – but good support players are just as important.

So I played good support. When I had the ball, I flew up the pitch with it. And when I didn't, I was always about to steal it, or waiting ready to pick up a pass. I even passed to Laurie and let him get a second goal.

The problem was, the other team were decent too. Not the 'complete shower' Jez had said. They'd been playing together longer and had their tactics all worked out. Their players moved together like pieces of the same machine – all connected, functioning like one.

When the ball was up their end, Laurie and me owned them. But it almost never was. And Leroy was struggling as captain. He spent most of the time waiting for other people to tell him what to do.

So I did. I took over tactics, and pretty soon the game started revolving around me in the same natural way it always seemed to focus on Freddie when he played. Except I was better. I was everywhere on the pitch – calling for passes, getting our defence to hold their lines. I'd never thought I could be a captain before, but it suddenly seemed easy. The game went the way I told it to.

The next time the ball made it to our side of the centre line, Leroy ran for it. He passed left, to where Laurie was waiting, but the other team were marking him. They were on him in a second, just like I knew they would be.

And I knew Laurie too. He wouldn't pass to me if his life depended on it, even if it meant giving the ball away. I watched my plan running like clockwork as they surrounded him, and he kicked the ball backwards rather than anywhere I could pick it up.

What Laurie hadn't noticed was Leroy joining the hustlers from the other team's defence, just like I'd whispered to him to try. When Laurie abandoned the ball, Leroy got it, and he had a clear shot to me.

And I had a clear shot to goal. I had enough space surrounding me to take my time shooting, but the keeper was watching me. I knew he'd be ready.

The whole game came down to just us, locking eyes across the line. He blinked. I kicked.

The keeper went the wrong way. He dived left. I'd kicked right, and my fist bunched up ready to punch the air as it soared for the top-right corner of the goal and . . .

Missed.

It missed. I'd done everything right. I'd practically played every position on the team for the last quarter of the match, but I hadn't been able to pull it back. Striking was what I was best at. But I'd missed.

And Jez was walking towards me with a face like thunder.

THIRTY-ONE

'What on earth did you think you were playing at?' Jez growled. The other team were celebrating with their coach as we all gathered round. Jez looked like he was about to rip my head off. 'Scratch that – what game did you even think you were playing? Because that wasn't football, Kershaw. Football's a team sport.'

That wasn't fair. Was it? Maybe I'd taken over a bit, but only because we'd been losing. Completely floundering against the opposition. Leroy had been totally lost until I'd stepped in.

'I was trying to get things back on our side.'

'Not your job,' Jez snapped. 'Are you the captain? No. Then why were you acting like it? And a bad captain too.'

My mouth fell open and stayed that way, wordless. I didn't understand. It felt like I'd been playing the game of my life.

'If you'd defended Laurie, he might have got his hat trick and brought us a tie. You let him get taken down so you could have the glory. I repeat, what kind of game do you think you're playing?'

That wasn't fair. Laurie hadn't been playing a team game, either. At least I hadn't actually *tackled him* for the ball. It was true, though, that I'd thought if I could just get one shot at goal – if I could just score – Jez would have had to let me start for the match tomorrow. I was focused on myself, not the team.

'I'm sorry – I was—'

Jez cut me off, snarling, 'You're right, you're sorry. A sorry excuse for a footballer. A sorry, snivelling little substitute. I never should have let you off the bench – we'd have had a better team playing a man down. Think you're a big man, do you?'

He stepped up to me, nearly half a foot taller and almost twice as broad. I didn't feel big, then. It was probably the smallest I'd ever felt.

'Think you're talented? A couple of lucky kicks, and you think you've got man of the match sewn up? You're not big, Kershaw. You're just a pathetic little loser. Have fun watching the match tomorrow, because that's where you belong. Lost in the crowd.'

Jez stormed off to offer the other coach some reluctant congratulations, and the rest of the team started to slowly drift away. Chidi caught my eye for a moment, then looked away, as if he was embarrassed for me.

I couldn't move, not yet. My legs felt shaky. My brain was telling me to run for it, just get out of there and never come back. But the way I was feeling, I'd have fallen over and humiliated myself more. If that were even possible.

The last person to go was Leroy. I looked up to find him staring at me, lips thinned out to a narrow, worried line.

'That wasn't necessary . . .' he started.

'No, it was. I messed up, Leroy. You were the captain, not me. I shouldn't have tried to take over everything.'

'Maybe not *everything*,' he said. 'It was a little bit too much. But if that shot had gone in, it would have been brilliant.'

I managed something that felt almost like a smile, but painful at the same time. 'Yeah. I'm sorry, though. For not waiting to find out how brilliant *your* ideas could have been.'

'Oh, I didn't have any,' he said honestly. 'But maybe one would have turned up from somewhere. I do play better under pressure.'

He clapped me on the back, and somehow it gave me the impetus to start to move, slowly, towards the dugout. Lacey was taking selfies with the two security guards who'd been trying not to stare at her all match, but Freddie and Kayla were waiting for us. From the strange shade of purple Kayla's face had turned, I could guess they'd heard everything Jez said.

I couldn't even look at Freddie.

'Thanks for the chance,' I said to my bootlaces instead. 'Think I might have messed it up.'

'It wasn't so bad.' Freddie's voice reassured me. All I could see was his socks. 'You might have started a new version of the game. Five-a-side getting old? Try one-versus-eleven.'

He was trying to be nice, I knew, but my face was burning too hot to really acknowledge it. I just wanted to dunk my head in a barrel of water and preferably never emerge.

'We'll wait outside,' Leroy murmured to Kayla, and he and Freddie left us alone.

'Of all the useless, talentless, unbelievable *idiots*,' she started, as soon as they'd gone. 'What a wet wipe. What a total, total waste of oxygen.'

I pushed my hands up over my face, feeling the flush against my palms. 'I know I messed up, but that's a bit harsh.'

'Not *you*,' Kayla snapped. 'That gorilla wearing the shirt that says *Coach*. Not that I think he can read it, because he certainly doesn't understand what it means. Coaches are supposed to build their teams *up*, Dylan, not stamp them into a fine powder under their heels.'

It was nice that she was defending me, but I shook my head. 'He was right. I tried to take over when we should have been playing as a team. It was my fault.'

'It was *his* fault for making that your only chance to prove yourself. No wonder you thought you had to do the work of a whole team – Freddie told me today's been the first chance you've really had to play.'

'Well . . . sort of.'

'It's been four days! And your dad's been paying for this. If he wanted you to spend a week running in circles, he could have sent you into the garden with a Frisbee. Why didn't you *tell* him you weren't being allowed to play tomorrow? Why didn't you tell *me*?'

'I thought you'd think I messed it all up.' I shifted uncomfortably where I stood, finally managing to look up at her. 'Or you'd pretend you didn't, and that would feel worse. *I* think I messed it all up.'

'Because that's what Jez Dutton's been telling you?'

I shrugged. 'Sort of.'

Kayla growled. Actually growled. If I'd been a small prey animal, I'd have been running by now. As it was, I felt somehow safer with her.

'Dylan, he can't even handle his dinner, let alone a football team. Lacey's been telling us a few things about him that you should probably know. But I think the most important one is that there are just some people who make themselves feel better by making sure everyone else feels worse. Did I ever tell you about the time Dad and I stayed with my aunt?'

I shook my head. She beckoned me over to the bench in the dugout, and we sat down. Out of the corner of my eye, I could see Lacey and Jez having some kind of argument as they both left the pitch. I hoped he wasn't taking anything out on her.

'What about your aunt?' I asked.

'It wasn't long after Mum left,' Kayla said.

Her mum had been out of the picture since before I'd known Kayla and her dad, but I knew she sometimes sent them postcards from far-off places – a different one every time. I knew none of them ever said, *Wish you were here.*

I reached for her hand as she took a deep breath and went on.

'Anyway, I spent a long time wondering if Mum leaving was my fault. If I just hadn't been enough for her to want to stay around for. And I think my aunt could sense weakness, the way sharks can spot blood in the water. She spent the whole visit constantly needling me about my weight. Telling me what to eat, what not to eat. Tutting every time I opened my mouth, let alone put anything in it. She'd written, *Reminder: Nothing Tastes as Good as Skinny Feels* at the top of every day on the wall calendar, and she told me it would help keep me focused on what was important.'

Kayla had always been plus-sized. She used to say she never grew out of the chubby baby phase, so she decided to make it work for her. And Kayla was easily the most beautiful girl I knew, but her aunt might as well have written *Reminder: You're Not OK as You Are* right there on her calendar.

I winced. 'How awful.'

Kayla shook her head, hard. 'How *sad* that that's what was most important to her. Not how loved she was, not how much she loved other people, only how much of her there was. And skinny isn't even a feeling – just like you can't actually *feel* fat. All you can do is feel good about yourself or bad about yourself. Imagine feeling bad just because you take up a few extra inches in the world? I'm generally a nice person, so those are pretty good inches. That's when I decided to choose to feel positive about being who I am, whatever size. No one gets to use me as a weapon against myself.'

'Did you tell your aunt that?' I asked.

'No.' She smirked. 'I just found her secret Cadbury's stash and glued the empty wrappers to the calendar pages before we left.'

I laughed. I couldn't help myself. Even if I was still feeling sort of wretched, she'd poured cool water on the worst of the burning, shameful parts. That was why she was my best friend. I wrapped an arm round her shoulder and tugged her in close. 'You're some of my favourite inches.'

She laughed and squirmed away. 'And you're mine. But – ugh – you weren't just playing enough for a whole team; you're sweating enough for one too. Please take a shower before we go.'

Shoving her lightly, I stood and shook myself off like a dog before heading to get changed.

THIRTY-TWO

I got showered and dressed as quickly as I could. We had the afternoon free, just in time to get to Kayla's final Ghoulish Games challenge – a live event being held in St Peter's Square in the city centre. I hadn't even had a chance to ask her what she planned to do for it.

Shouldering my way out of the changing room, I expected to find her waiting for me. But she wasn't.

Freddie was.

I was starting to find the existence of Freddie Alton pretty unfair. At least, the fact that he kept existing so near me. And that I'd had to watch him play football all week, which, even if it wasn't what he wanted to do forever, looked exactly like what he should be doing right now. He looked like a magazine advert selling perfect players – somehow, he could run around a pitch for hours without breaking a sweat, let alone picking up bruises or grazed knees. My legs looked like I'd just gone for a run through a patch of barbed wire, and I'd hardly even played.

He wasn't completely flawless, obviously. It wasn't like he had hair that never fell out of place. It was just that every new place it fell into looked as good as the last one. And I knew now what it was about his eyes I'd always liked.

They were kind. He had kind eyes and a kind smile and a face that could make me feel a little bit dizzy if I stared at him for too long. He wouldn't be short of patients if he did become a doctor. People would be swooning all over the place as soon as he walked in wearing a white coat.

And I was stuck being near him all the time, trying not to think about all the things I liked about him or to wonder what things he might like about me. I knew that if I started, then I might not stop, and things in my life were complicated enough without giving myself more reasons to feel guilty.

I still didn't even know if I had a boyfriend to feel guilty about.

At least I was pretty sure I'd learned how to talk normally when Freddie was around. Then I opened my mouth, and Mickey Mouse squealed out a 'Hi!'

Honestly, it was like dealing with my voice breaking all over again, and that had been traumatic enough the first time. I'd stopped answering the phone when my voice got too unpredictable, because people kept thinking I was my mum.

Freddie didn't let on if he'd noticed my uncanny

Disney impression. 'Hey. So Kayla told me she set you straight about how unfair that was back there.'

My lips twisted. She had, but . . . Jez had made some sense too. 'It wasn't *all* unfair.'

'It is when you realize he's had you set up from the start,' Freddie said darkly.

From the start? It was true that Jez had been coming down on me hard the whole week, and I'd never understood why. 'I must have done something to cause it. I just don't know what.'

'You did. You messed it up in your first half an hour.'

'I did?'

Freddie nodded. 'Remember those practice penalties on your first day?'

That didn't make sense. 'But those all went in? That's what I'm good at.'

'Exactly. It took you five minutes to demonstrate to Jez that you were the biggest threat here, and he's been working on keeping you out of action ever since.'

I squinted at Freddie, not really seeing it.

'Lacey told me. She says he always picks on the biggest talent, and this week he's being especially bad because of the match at the end of the week. Pros versus students. Don't you think it's weird that Jez is captaining the team playing *against* us when he's supposed to be *our* coach?'

'I just thought that was how it worked . . .'

To be honest, I hadn't thought about it at all. Now that I did, it did seem strange. Chidi had said there might be scouts to impress, but we thought they'd be coming to check out the students, not the coach. Everybody already knew Jez could play – he'd never been a legend on the field, but he'd been talented enough. So why play *against* us when his job was to get us playing our best? To use some of Kayla's legal speak, it sounded like a conflict of interests.

Freddie had obviously thought so too. 'Jez wants to use this match to get out of amateur coaching, for good. He wants to be the star of the match so people remember how good he was before the curry incident killed his career. Then maybe he can get back to playing for a few more years in a lower-league team.'

I stared at Freddie as we walked down the hall, and for once I wasn't wondering how anyone's nose could be quite so ideally shaped for their face. 'So he's using us to make himself look good?' It was just like Kayla had said. 'Why did Lacey tell you all this?'

Freddie smiled. 'We get on really well. You know, there really is a lot more to her than meets the eye.'

That wasn't what the gossip magazines said, but they were usually talking about the cut of her dresses.

'We were talking about her PhD. She hasn't told Jez

about it because he doesn't like the idea of his girlfriend being more intelligent than he is – which means he shouldn't be dating anyone able to feed and dress themselves, as far as I'm concerned. But she said he's the same way about football. Look at his record and see how much time the best players in his teams spent out injured.'

I could hardly believe what I was hearing. 'Why is Lacey still dating him, then?'

'They met at school. She says he was all right back then, but success went to his head. Maybe all that curry overheated his brain. Anyway, she's telling him about the PhD tonight.'

'That must have been what they were arguing about.' I sighed. 'Well, it's not going to save me from the subs bench tomorrow, but at least now I understand why I'll be there.'

Freddie nodded. 'I'm sorry it's so unfair. Leroy says he's going to write a scathing Twitter review of the course.'

I grinned. 'Maybe I should do that too: *Delighted to say Feet of the Future is firmly in my past. One star – would not attend again.*'

'I would,' Freddie said quietly.

'Seriously? You don't even like football that much.'

'Not really.' He shrugged. 'But I like you, so it's been worth it.'

This was it. My chance to tell him I liked him too. That I'd liked him for ages, long before I'd actually spoken to him. I'd liked him even when I'd thought he must be a complete jerk, because no one could possibly be allowed to be as attractive as he was and be nice.

I really did like him. But it was strange. All that time I'd spent at school imagining what it would be like if he were my boyfriend, I'd never once imagined us as *friends*.

My phone buzzed in my pocket. I pulled it out, and this time didn't bother to hide the photo of Leo on my screen. I still hung up without answering, though.

Freddie was watching. 'Do you ever actually speak to him? Your boyfriend?'

I looked away. 'I don't know if I want to, yet.'

We turned the corner towards the doors to find Kayla and Leroy waiting.

'We're not late for the contest, are we?' I asked.

'It wouldn't matter if we were,' Kayla said. Her jaw looked oddly tight. 'I've got nothing to enter in it.'

'What?' I'd seen her drag in a full bag of supplies this morning. It couldn't have evaporated – though she wasn't holding it now. 'But you were picked to go along tonight! You've been working on it all week!'

'I know, but it's all gone. We're supposed to go down there and give them a big scare – I'd been turning that cheerleader outfit into an evil zombie chainsaw cheerleader . . . It was going to be a great costume; I'd even made a backdrop to go with it. And I was going to get one of you to let me cut them up onstage, but . . .'

She stopped, her jaw setting tight.

'The cleaners must have been in the office this morning,' Leroy finished. 'Seen all the ripped cloth and bloodstained mannequin parts and thrown them out.'

'So I've got nothing to show,' Kayla said. 'And there's no time to come up with anything else. That was my best idea, anyway.'

'Don't be ridiculous – we must be able to think of something,' I said urgently. I couldn't let Kayla get relegated to the subs bench too.

We all stared at each other blankly.

Then Leroy said, 'I think I might have an idea.'

And by the time he'd finished telling us what it was, it was him we were all staring at.

He smiled shyly. 'I told you I was good under pressure.'

THIRTY-THREE

We had to jog from the bus stop to reach St Peter's Square in time. Freddie and I were both on our phones, while Kayla and Leroy were dragging a huge bag between them. I could hear the crowd before I saw it. The Deathsplash Nightmares weren't even attending, but I recognized half the fans that had been staking out our hotel among the faces.

Up onstage, a group of boys about our age were holding a CD player with a sign dangling from it reading *World's Loudest Scream*. Since the crowd were already drowning out the sound it made, I didn't think they had much of a shot at the prize for a 'big scare'.

My phone kept buzzing. Texts were coming in quicker than I could reply to them – half from unknown numbers. I added them all to a group chat on my phone and sent a quick message.

We're here. Look for the girl with the green hair.

I eyed Kayla and realized the problem with using her as a marker point. Her hair was bright enough to stand out, but she was barely five feet tall in heels – there was no point looking for her in a crowd when she was hidden in the depths of it.

Freddie must have got my message and had the same thought. I looked at him, then said, 'Kayla, crouch down.'

'What? Why?' She abandoned the handle of the bag she was sharing with Leroy, and he struggled for a moment before dropping it, panting.

'Just do it!'

She crouched. I bent forward on one knee, and Freddie picked her up and set her firmly on my shoulders. He held her hand as I shakily straightened up.

Seconds later, the first person came up to us. She had an absurdly bright smile and dozens of coloured beads woven into her box braids, and she still had her Camp Cheer uniform on. 'Dylan and Kayla? I'm Cindy, the cheer captain. We're here for the scare.'

Onstage, the final entry before ours was being played, and it was a good one. The Deathsplash Nightmares' hit 'RIP ROCKNROLL' started up with a low, menacing beat, a music video accompanying it on a big screen. The usual live footage of the Nightmares in concert was intercut with a horror movie, making it look like the crowd were a bunch of zombies who'd started to hunt each other for brains. It almost looked professionally made.

'Oh, no, this is amazing . . .' Kayla leaned down

and murmured into my ear.

'I think we're still in with a chance. Come on – we'd better get to the stage.'

Almost everyone we'd called had shown up in time. Josh, Chidi, Aaron and most of Feet of the Future – and, thanks to Freddie having phone numbers for a few of the cheer squad, they'd all turned up too. In total, there were nearly twenty of us getting ready at the edge of the stage.

Leroy handed out hideous pull-on plastic masks from his bag – corpses, monsters and American presidents – while Cindy told us exactly where we had to stand. She was working Kayla and the football team into one of the big routines they'd be performing tomorrow. As soon as the video onstage ended – and the applause died down – the cheerleaders ran on wearing the horror masks and shaking their pom-poms.

'Give us an S!'

Already worked up, the crowd yelled back happily, 'S!'

'Give us a C!'

'C!'

'Give us an A!'

'A!'

'Give us an R!'

'R!'

'Give us an E!'

'E!'

'What does it spell?'

The crowd yelled back at us, 'SCARE!'

Me, Freddie and the rest of the team moved on to the stage to the spots we'd been given, taking up support positions. I'd started to regret being so enthusiastic about Leroy's idea – I couldn't even catch a ball, let alone a person flying through the air. All I could think about was tomorrow's 'Cheer Carnage' headlines, with a photo of me dropping Cindy on her head.

But there was no going back now. Thankfully I wasn't given too much time to worry, because as soon as we were in our places, the cheer squad started leaping and backflipping into theirs.

It's a good word, SCARE. It's full of clean, simple lines. I'd just never expected to have to *become* it before.

I was in the middle, the backbone of the R. All I had to do was stand solidly and hold on to the waist of a girl I'd never met before, who was climbing on to my shoulders.

'I'm Nishi,' she whispered, as she set her feet on either side of my neck. 'Nice to meet you!'

Then she bent over backwards, trusting me to hold on to her as she curved her spine and grabbed me by my waist to form the top part of the R. One of the male cheerleaders lay on the floor with his feet flat against my stomach to be the lower section.

All along the row, everyone was settling into their positions. *E* was formed by Freddie and Chidi working together to hold up a girl with her legs and arms straight out at right angles.

There was a murmuring from the crowd as they worked out what we were doing, and then finally a burst of applause. It was cheesy, but it couldn't be denied: we'd given them a really big *SCARE*.

We held the positions until my legs were starting to buckle – as a photographer from the local press darted out to get a picture. Then gradually the *SCARE* fell apart. Cheerleaders jumped up and punched the air. Nishi took a bow from my shoulders before climbing down. As they celebrated, some of them started doing flips on the spot. Cindy did a cartwheel before another cheerleader caught her and helped flip her into the air. She spun round twice before someone else caught her.

Then another girl tried it. In a minute, it seemed like the air was full of flying girls. We formed a circle, clapping, and the crowd started to join in as the cheer squad took turns to do ever more impressive leaps and throws. Finally Cindy and one of the male cheerleaders threw a girl incredibly high, right in the middle of the circle.

She spun in the air, a mix of bright uniform and green hair, then came down.

And nobody caught her.

We were in such a close huddle by then that her fall couldn't be seen, but there was a thud and crack as she hit the stage, and . . . silence.

Even the crowd fell silent.

You could have heard a whisper a mile away, it was so quiet. We'd all rushed forward, pressing in around the girl where she fell . . . until other people started to fall forward too. Or to be dragged down by some irresistible force. People – from the cheer squad and from our team too – were tumbling forward, on to their faces, on to hands and knees, and nobody was getting back up. It wasn't long before I was one of them, dragged down into the pile, unmoving.

Until finally, over the pyramid of fallen bodies, Kayla the zombie cheerleader crawled her way out.

She'd still had the make-up she'd been planning to use, and we'd borrowed a uniform so she'd fit in with the others. Aaron – who'd be in goal tomorrow and was a thousand times better than me at catching anything – had been instructed to dive forward and catch Kayla as she fell. Chidi had made the thudding noise that sounded like her hitting the stage.

The crowd went completely nuts. When I finally got

back up, Kayla was grinning like a zombie in a Mensa meeting.

The local DJ whose radio station was running the competition rushed forward to grab her hands and introduce her to the crowd. 'Kayla Flores, everyone!' she said into her mic. 'I don't know about you, but she nearly gave me a heart attack! And that's all our entries. Now, let's get everyone up here, and we'll let the judges give their verdict.'

The way the crowd were screaming for Kayla, it was already settled as far as I was concerned. There was no way she wouldn't win now.

THIRTY-FOUR

'I can't *believe* you didn't win,' Leroy muttered, shaking his head. He was watching Kayla, clearly worried.

We all were. The crowds had dispersed pretty quickly after the contest was over, some of them coming up to tell Kayla she'd been robbed, or that she'd definitely scared *them* the most. She'd managed to nod and smile politely for a while, but she'd been staring silently into space for half an hour now, clutching the bag of Deathsplash Nightmares merchandise she'd won for coming in second place to the music video. She wasn't even eating the pizza Freddie had picked up as a consolation dinner, just staring and twitching slightly when someone said the words *win* or *second* or *tiebreak*.

'I can't believe you came second. In a tiebreak!' Leroy said, for about the eighth time in the last ten minutes.

I put a hand on his shoulder. 'All right, I think she's got that you can't believe it,' I said. 'The problem is, it's true.'

'And now you're not going to get to see the concert!' Leroy added. 'You might as well have stayed at home and watched YouTube clips on your phone!'

Next to me, Freddie groaned. 'You know what, Leroy – we'd better head off,' he said, tossing a piece of pizza crust back into the box and standing up. 'Big day tomorrow. You want to make sure you're captaining on an early night.'

'Or maybe I shouldn't sleep at all?' Leroy suggested. 'I do seem to do well un—'

'Under pressure. We know.' I wasn't sure that insomnia would suddenly turn Leroy into a tactical mastermind, but he'd surprised us once today. 'Listen, did you sleep last night?'

He gave me a quizzical look. 'Yes?'

'Then you don't need to get less sleep to have good ideas. You should probably try to get exactly the same amount as you had last night.'

'Good plan,' Freddie put in.

'Well, I suppose I shouldn't leave Mum waiting much longer, anyway,' Leroy said, finally standing. 'Anyone need a lift?'

'What do you mean, *waiting*?' I asked.

'Oh, she's in the car over there.'

He pointed to a green car parked up in a bay at the side of the street. If I squinted, I could just make out an *I HEART WALES* sticker in the window. A woman squinted back at me as I stared.

'She doesn't like me to go off on my own in strange

225

places,' Leroy said. 'So she followed us from the training centre.'

Freddie looked dazed. 'But why was she there? You take a bus.'

'Well, she follows the bus too,' Leroy replied, as if that were obvious. 'She doesn't want to disrupt my social development, just to make sure I'm not kidnapped.'

I looked at him. Freddie looked at him. Even Kayla slowly lifted her head to look at him miserably.

Finally, Freddie nodded. 'Yeah . . . OK, Leroy. You can give me a lift.'

Slowly they headed off together across the street.

'I've called Mum and Dad,' I told Kayla. 'They're on their way. You don't have to pretend in front of them – we'll just tell them you're miserable because you couldn't find anything nice at the shops.'

'I'm not miserable,' Kayla said, hunching over to wrap her arms round her knees.

I shifted closer, bumping her shoulder with mine. 'No? Could have fooled me.'

She sighed. 'It's just . . . it feels like the wrong ending. Like I should have won because I put so much work into winning. I should have won because I talked my way into coming here with you, and I've been sneaking around the whole week, and I've worked *so* hard. That's how these things are supposed to go.'

It was true. If someone made the film of our lives, one day in the future, with the currently infant children of famous movie stars playing our parts, they'd definitely change this bit so Kayla would emerge victorious. But, since we weren't currently living in the film version, I couldn't ask for a rewrite. 'Sometimes things don't happen the way they're supposed to.'

'But there's more than that,' she said. 'We should have won because we overcame disaster and pulled it off with teamwork. That's the moral of half the stories I read as a child: you can do anything if you work together. What's the *point* of stories having morals if they aren't even true? How do we know *all* happy endings won't turn out to be lies?'

Her bleak mood was getting infectious. I was starting to think about the happy endings I'd been taking for granted – like the happy ending Leo and I had to our holiday romance. 'Maybe they will. But . . .'

I bit my lip and trailed off to think. I wasn't sure Leo and I were going to have a happy ending any more. But when that *was* what I expected, all I did was worry that something was about to mess it up.

'But even if your happy ending might not happen, it's still worth trying for, isn't it? You didn't win today, but if we'd given up and gone home after your first idea didn't work out, you'd never even have had a chance.'

'Maybe it would have been better not to have had a chance. I wouldn't have got my hopes up.' Kayla scuffed her feet against the step we were sitting on and reached across to grab the last slice of pizza.

'I don't think so,' I said. I wasn't sure about it, yet, but I couldn't help thinking that chances were what kept people going. Even ones that might not work out. 'I think maybe stories only really end unhappily when you give up. If you keep trying, there's always a chance to fix them.'

'It doesn't seem like there are many chances left to fix this,' Kayla said.

'Well, the band *are* staying in our hotel. Alonzo's probably filled Rick's room with a series of tripwires and booby traps after our visit the other day, but there's still a chance to catch him at the breakfast buffet.'

From somewhere, Kayla managed to find half a smile. 'I told you, rock stars don't do buffets.'

'Or hamsters.'

'Just hot dogs and Abba,' Kayla said. 'I can't believe that's what he listens to!'

'Same as my mum.' I grinned. 'Maybe she's missing out on her true calling as a death-metal artist. You should hear her scream at me when I don't hang up the towels.'

There was a real smile on Kayla's face now. 'All right, all right – I'll give not giving up a chance. But you have

228

to give something a chance too.'

I raised an eyebrow. 'Like what?'

'Like Leo. And don't ask me how I know something's wrong. You weren't wearing that stupid smile you always get after you talk to him this morning, and now you're ignoring his calls.'

She was some sort of wizard, honestly. 'But how do you *know* that?'

She tapped the side of my coat where it was pressed up against her. 'Your pocket's been vibrating all night.'

THIRTY-FIVE

The next morning, I got up early and curled up on the sofa to check my messages from Leo. Last night, there had been too much going on

But now I had to make myself read what Leo had sent me. I'd ignored him for a whole day without really having a reason. Not one I was sure about, anyway. So now I was expecting the inevitable: a series of messages letting me down gently. Saying he was sorry, but he was having more fun with other people, and that maybe we should just break it off.

Instead, I scrolled through a list of messages that were getting more and more worried. They started with

> Hey, I must have missed your call.
> Everything good?

And progressed to

> Are you there?

> Can I call?

> Hey, we just broke for lunch.
> Still haven't heard from you.

And finally

> Dylan, just let me know you
> got this, please. Please?

I should have answered his messages or picked up when he called yesterday. He'd spent the whole day trying to check I was all right just because I missed our usual telephone date.

I hadn't even realized it, because they weren't the type of dates where you held hands, or took long romantic walks, or shared plates of spaghetti so huge that you kissed in the middle of a pasta strand, but maybe we'd been dating all along. Not the way it was supposed to happen, but *our* way. Every day, we'd met up for at least a few minutes on the phone.

Until I'd stood him up.

The last messages had been sent late last night.

> I called your dad. He said you were sleeping and
> you're probably stressed about the match. You
> shouldn't be. I know I can't be there, and I know
> Kayla's not into it, but I'm your biggest cheerleader,

OK? So just picture me with pom-poms,
and you'll be fine. Promise.
Talk tomorrow, I hope.
Miss you.

I'd been so stupid. No matter what else he was doing,
or who he was with, he always took the time for me.
Looking at his number on my phone, I held my breath,
and pressed call.

Then listened to it ring and ring at Leo's end.

No one answered.

And for once, my brain told me it was probably
because it was 7 a.m., and not because he was ignoring
me to have his morning muesli with a chorus line of
imaginary dancers. I sent a message instead.

Hey. I'm sorry about yesterday. I'll tell you
about it soon. This morning's going to be a
bit mad, but I promise I'll call when it's all
over. You never told me, by the way, when
your big show's on? Or what it is, exactly?
Miss you too.

I hoped the messages would be the first thing he'd see
when he woke up.

Then I hoped the messages didn't *wake* him up. I

couldn't cope if I'd made him spend the day sleep-deprived. What if he got dizzy in the middle of a pirouette and ended up snapping some important dancing bone?

On second thoughts, I really should have sent an email instead.

After a few minutes without getting a text back reading **OW, OW, MY LEG, MY BEAUTIFUL, PERFECT, VITAL-FOR-MY-FUTURE-CAREER-PLANS LEG**, I let myself relax a bit.

The next message I had was from Leroy, who hopefully hadn't been awake all night trying out his insomnia plan. I smiled to myself after reading it and tapped out a reply.

Then I looked up, startled, as the room door opened. Jude dived towards the sofa on his Rollator, with Dad in hot pursuit. They must have been down to the first sitting at breakfast – Jude liked going early so he could pick out all the best Coco Pops. His face was raspberry-red, though, and I knew he only turned varying shades of fruit when he was upset.

'What's happened?' I asked, catching him as he threw his arms out towards me and lifting him on to the sofa at my side. 'Ghost in the dining room again? You know it was probably only Dad making a spooktacle of himself.'

The pun fell flat, although the weary look Dad gave me suggested he appreciated the effort.

Jude buried his face against my shoulder, sniffing sadly, and I didn't even complain when I realized he was using my pyjama shirt to wipe his nose. When you live with a five-year-old, everything ends up sticky at some point.

'There's no such *thing* as ghosts,' Jude sputtered out. 'The lady in reception says so. She says people always ask about it, and she doesn't know why anyone gets so excited about things that aren't even real.'

'But isn't that a good thing?' I slung an arm round Jude. 'I've been telling you ghosts don't exist for ages.'

Dad's expression warned me I'd wandered into dangerous territory, but it was too late now. I could feel fresh sobs welling up in Jude again.

'*No*, because, because . . . it means . . .'

I waited as he drew in a deep, trembly breath.

'*Because it means I'll never see Fluffy again!*'

I froze. First, because Dad wasn't supposed to know that Fluffy was with us in the hotel, whether in spirit or not. Second, because I had a sudden chilly feeling that the ratbusters must have caught up with Jude's hamster.

One thing at a time. I'd deal with telling Dad later – first, I had to find out if Fluffy was on that heavenly hamster wheel Kayla had been so worried about. 'What has Fluffy got to do with ghosts? Do you think he's seen one? Has all his fur turned white?'

That would make buying a secret replacement hamster a lot easier. Jude shook his head firmly, pointing back to the door.

'He's outside. We saw him, and now I'll never see him again.'

'What do you mean he's outside? In the hall?'

Confused, I looked across at Dad, who just shrugged.

'Go and look.'

I went and looked. Outside in the hallway, Rick Deathsplash was propped up against the door of his own hotel room, wearing a fake-fur coat. A fake-fur coat covered in splotches of purple and white . . . and orange.

And I thought I understood. I looked back at Jude for a moment, then headed out to introduce myself to the lead singer of the Deathsplash Nightmares, again.

'Uh, Rick?'

He forced his eyes open and looked blearily across at me.

'I mean, um, Mr Nightmares? Is everything all right?'

Rick took a moment to reply, probably weighing up whether or not I was enough of a crazed fan to be stalking the corridors at all times of the day waiting to pounce on him, or whether I really was just another hotel guest. Finally he seemed to decide he could talk to me – pressing the back of his palm to his forehead in a dramatic swoon. 'I just wanted to go to the vending machine – is that such a crime?'

'Um, no?' I tried, not expecting complicated legal questions this early in the morning. 'I mean a boy at our school got his arm stuck in the tray trying to get a free Mars bar once. They had to call the fire brigade during maths, and they told *him* it was a crime, but he was never arrested or anything.'

The rock god held up an empty packet of Pom-Bears. 'Men have needs. But desire will lead to your downfall. Remember that.'

'I'll make a note.' I scribbled an imaginary one on my palm, which seemed to satisfy him. 'But why are you out here?'

'Alonzo's security system.' Rick sighed. 'All geniuses are flawed somehow. It's locked me out.'

I could see my chance, even if I couldn't believe he'd actually take it. 'Well, you look very tired. And don't you have a concert tonight too?'

Rick nodded wearily.

'Then you should come and nap on our sofa,' I said firmly. 'At least until Alonzo wakes up and undoes the padlocks.'

'Your sofa . . .' Rick said, as if it were an alien concept. He looked up the hallway to where light was flooding out from our door. 'You don't live with that crying child, do you?'

He tucked his arms around his chest, looking like an oversized anxious tortoiseshell cat. One wearing a genuine-looking pout. 'Children never seem to like me. I can't understand why.'

It might have been all the screamy songs about the inevitability of death, and the fact that he had a spider tattooed on his face, but that was just a guess. I didn't want to be judgemental. 'I think I know how you can make this one like you. He's my brother.'

Rick looked at me dubiously for a moment, then nodded. 'Lead the way.'

When I walked through the door with Rick Deathsplash, both Jude and my dad made exactly the same yelping noise. Jude looked like he was ready to wail again, so I had to jump in fast.

'Jude, this is Mr Deathsplash Nightmares, and he's very tired. I told him he could sit on our sofa for a bit, but first he has to tell you his coat's not made of hamsters.'

'*Hamsters?*' Rick looked genuinely offended at the idea. 'Little boy, like my life, all my fashion is *cruelty free*. This coat was crafted by elderly Italian nuns. The fibres are made from recycled plastic bags collected by a charity I personally sponsor to retrieve them from the sea. This coat does more *good* than harm. It is not your hamster.'

'Besides,' I added, 'did you ever see a purple one?'

Jude shook his head slowly. I could see him trying to figure out whether or not everything Rick had said added up to a good thing.

'It's a fake-fur coat, Jude,' I said. 'Not real. Fluffy's alive and well and living . . . somewhere that definitely isn't this hotel.'

Dad and Rick both looked at me as I cleared my throat.

'And now Rick can sit down.'

Rick curled up at the end of the couch without further invitation, stretching his hand-made, recycled, elderly nun fake-fur coat across him for a blanket. Dad was still sitting on the coffee table, blinking between me and the rock star on his sofa.

And Dad always did think it was rude to invite someone in without making small talk.

'So,' he started, just as Rick looked like he might be about to drift to sleep. 'I'm Dylan's dad, Nick Kershaw. And where are you from?'

Rick Deathsplash opened one green eye and fixed it on him. 'I live inside my own heart, Nick Kershaw,' he said, and then he passed out against the cushions.

Which looked a lot more comfortable than the floor Kayla passed out on when she came out of her room a few minutes later.

THIRTY-SIX

Kayla swore she'd fallen over in surprise, not actually fainted at the sight of a rock god on the sofa, but we both knew the truth. She'd recovered pretty quickly, though, and had sat watching Rick as he slept, loudly hushing anyone who made the slightest noise to disturb him. It meant me and Dad had to have 'the conversation' about Fluffy out in the hall.

'We should have told you, but you were so sure Grandma had lost him at home. I thought it didn't really matter *where* he was missing, just that we got him back. Jude knew where he was.'

Dad raised his eyebrows. 'Your brother thought he'd been turned into a coat.'

'Well, to be honest, the getting-him-back part hasn't been going all that well. But we've been trying! And once we didn't tell you on the first day . . .'

'It got harder and harder,' Dad finished.

I was relieved he seemed to understand. In fact, he looked a bit sheepish – scratching the back of his head and not quite making eye contact.

'Well, I can't really blame you when your mum and I

239

have been setting Jude up on Skype chats with a rented hamster all week.'

'Rented?'

'Your gran got one from a class pet-lending scheme at the local primary school. Bribed one of the kids. He has to go back when term starts, or the game'll be up.'

I whistled softly. 'Who knew Gran was a criminal mastermind. And you too – I can't believe you've had Jude chatting to a faux Fluffy.'

'I can't believe he knew it was a fake and never said a word,' Dad spluttered. 'Sneaky kid.'

We looked at each other. 'Must run in the family.'

While we were on the subject of secrets and lies, I realized this was the time to tell him not to bother coming to the match that afternoon. Jez was bound to do everything to stop me getting off the bench, and I didn't want Dad sitting there embarrassed to be supporting someone who sat on their bum for ninety minutes.

I just had to find a way of telling him about it that wouldn't result in him picketing the pitch in protest at the way Jez had acted. Maybe if I just started talking, the right words would somehow find themselves.

'Dad, I—'

Some people get saved by the bell when they've got bad news to deliver. I got saved by a long, anguished scream from down the hall.

Alonzo was standing in front of Rick's hotel room door, clutching a remote control that must have operated all the extra security features that kept Rick locked out last night.

'Empty . . .' he was muttering to himself, frantic. 'How can it be empty? Alonzo, you have lost a star. Kidnapped! Why! Why?' He flung himself against the door. 'So talented. So innocent. So pure. No, no. Please, let there be a miracle. Let them come back and take *me*!'

Dad cleared his throat.

Alonzo ignored him, beating his fists dramatically against the door.

So I put two fingers between my lips and whistled. It's one of my talents besides being decent at football: really, really loud whistles.

Actually, it was possible my talents were just the football and that. Maybe being good at both meant I had a future as a referee.

It made Alonzo look up, though. He narrowed his eyes at us, probably wondering where he'd seen my face before.

'Who are you?' he sniffed.

I grinned. 'Oh, just miracle workers.'

Kayla burst out of our hotel room door, her hands firmly set on her hips. 'Who made that terrible noise? Don't you know the world's most grammy-nominated

241

death-metal artiste has been trying to sleep in here?'

Alonzo rubbed the tears away from one eye, then the other. He blinked at Kayla. And then he broke into a run.

After an emotional reunion, Alonzo started to fuss Rick into going back to his own room. Meanwhile, Kayla was trying to fuss him into staying. I thought they might have an actual fight over it for a while, but she was finally persuaded to let him go – though only once he was clutching her sparkly pink travel cup full of fresh herbal tea 'for the journey'.

Rick looked genuinely touched by the gift.

'I'll remember this kindness. And I'll never forget *you*, Layla Flores.'

He drifted out into the hall. I stopped Alonzo for a second, before he could follow.

'So um, I don't suppose there's a chance of getting tickets for tonight? For services rendered to rock?'

Alonzo laughed, as if I'd just asked him to get me a piece of the moon. 'There is not – how you say – a snowball's chance in hell. The concert, it has been sold out for months. However, I will leave a bag of merchandise for you at reception, in gratitude.'

He trotted after Rick, dashing into his suite seconds before the door closed. From behind it, I could hear the sound of a dozen locks being set.

Nervously I turned back to Kayla. I wasn't sure if

meeting Rick this way had been exactly what she'd had in mind. 'How are you?'

She hugged herself, sighing happily. 'You were right – you should never give up on your dreams. Rick Deathsplash knows my name.'

I must have looked surprised.

'He knows *most* of my name,' she went on. 'It's near enough. And it may not have been quite the exchange of beautiful minds I wanted, but maybe an exchange of beautiful travel mugs is near enough.'

Humming something that might have been 'Dancing Queen', she took her own mug of tea and shimmied back towards her bedroom. Dad had gone to begin the slow and delicate process of waking Mum up without getting his head ripped off for it, which left me with Jude.

He'd stayed on the couch roughly where I'd left him, munching on a breakfast biscuit and watching episodes of *Twinkle the Talking Train* with the volume turned down so as not to disturb Rick when he slept. Jude knew the words to every episode already, so it wasn't too much of a sacrifice.

I settled in next to him, reaching over to break off a bit of his biscuit as he squirmed in protest.

'Haven't you already had breakfast?' I asked.

Jude pushed the rest of his snack into his mouth and spoke through the crumbs. 'Only *one*.'

243

'Well, I suppose you do need to keep your strength up. You've got a game today too.'

Whizzy Wheels were holding demonstration matches all day. Jude was in the youngest group, so he'd be up first that morning. It meant Dad could fit us both in.

'I wish I could come to yours. Want to know a secret?' I asked.

Jude nodded – he *loved* secrets.

'I think I'd rather be at your match than mine. But you have to do something for me, OK?'

Jude was still young enough to agree to things without worrying whether the question was a trap, so he nodded easily. 'You've got to play the best you ever have. Give Dad something to cheer about. And get him to video it so I can watch you later.'

'On the TV,' Jude said, perking up considerably. 'Just like Twinkle.'

I grinned. 'You've even got the wheels to match.'

He'd actually had a Twinkle the talking train Halloween costume made that incorporated his chair. It was one of the coolest things I'd ever seen. I was about to go and start getting ready, when Jude pulled my sleeve and kept me there.

'Dyl?'

'Yeah?'

'When will I get Fluffy back?'

Ooof. I sank back into the sofa cushions, trying not to make eye contact. At least if the hamster *had* been turned into a coat, we'd know what had happened to him. As it was, the only thing Fluffy was cloaked in was *mystery*.

'I don't know yet. We've been trying to find him, I promise. I know you wish you had him back and . . . I want you to have everything you wish for. Even if that would probably mean some crazy things, like crisps for every meal or a bed made of Lego. But even if I'm trying my hardest, I don't know if I can make every wish come true. We'll keep looking, OK?'

Jude's lip quivered, but he squeezed my hand and smiled.

I grinned back. 'Anything else?'

He paused for a minute, then said thoughtfully, 'I wish I could have another biscuit.'

Sneaky. It definitely runs in the family. 'Like I said, we don't just get everything we wish for.'

I ruffled his hair and stood up. It was definitely true. I didn't even know how I wished today would turn out any more. Sometimes you have to stop wishing for things and just let them happen instead.

THIRTY-SEVEN

The pre-match build-up at Feet of the Future meant there was a weird atmosphere in the training ground. Jez gave us a list of warm-ups and then left Laurie to run everyone through them while he worked with the team of 'old pros' – mostly league players who'd gotten a bit too old and slow. That didn't make them any less impressive, though. They'd played real matches, on actual TV, with proper commentators calling them rubbish and mispronouncing their names.

Most of our team were watching Jez's, making their own register of the players they recognized. It was enough to make anyone forget that *we* were actually supposed to be Jez's team.

The nerves were building in everyone. Chidi had stopped talking about the possibility of being scouted. In fact, he'd stopped talking at all, which was definitely a first. He was looking a little bit more ashen every time a new pro player walked through the doors.

Leroy was worrying too. 'Mum keeps saying I'll be the pride of the valleys,' he said with a gulp, joining me for some lunges and lifts.

'Maybe you will,' I told him. 'And if not, who except her is going to know?'

That seemed to make him more nervous somehow. Any other attempts at conversation were met with a wide-eyed stare.

I kept telling myself there was no point being afraid of what Dad would think: it was too late to change anything now. Kayla would probably end up telling him before I could, anyway. It wasn't just me who'd been keeping secrets that Mum and Dad were inevitably going to find out today – she still hadn't told them she wasn't a cheerleader.

In fact, since she wasn't cheerleading, and the Ghoulish Games contest was over, I wasn't totally sure where Kayla *was*. She had a new fake reason for being there – as Lacey Laine's personal assistant – but Lacey hadn't arrived yet, so there wasn't anything to assist with.

A small thread of worry twisting inside me, I waited until the last break before the match, and dashed down to the back offices to look for her.

There was no one there. I tried every door, but they were all locked. Even the secret locker shrine to our invented dead player had been taken down – which I thought was pretty disrespectful, actually. There was no sign of Kayla anywhere, even though I pressed my face so hard against the glass of the office she'd been using that it left a nose print.

'I'd been wondering where she was too,' Freddie said from behind me, startling me so much I tipped forward and left a forehead print on the glass to match the dot of my nose. I rubbed my temples as I turned round to squint at him.

'So you came to look for her?'

He smiled, rubbing his hand against the back of his slightly pinkish-looking neck. Was he *blushing*?

'No, Dylan. I came to look for you.'

'But I'm not lost; I've been on the pitch all morning. Though I don't know why I'm bothering to warm up for a hectic afternoon of sitting around *watching* football.'

Freddie took a step closer. 'No – I meant I came to find you because I wanted to catch you alone.'

I couldn't take a step anywhere. Freddie was right in front of me, and the office wall was at my back. He'd have moved if I'd wanted him to. It was just that I felt strangely frozen in place. 'I mean, from what I've seen people do on match days at Dad's pub, I should be warming up by developing a high tolerance for pork scratchings and practising my beer burps.'

I knew Freddie was trying to say something, but I just couldn't stop talking. It was like my mouth was Jude's toy cupboard, and what was coming out was rapid and unstoppable, like all the building blocks that fell on my head every time I opened it.

'I should be warming up by yelling about how blind the ref is and making a list of which swear words rhyme so I can make up chants about the opposition.'

Freddie was half smiling, but he looked somehow serious too. Intent. That was the word. He looked really *intent*.

'Then I can spend five minutes doing reps of scratching my bum and waving at a mate to fetch in another round of drinks. *That's* how I should be—'

The next words were going to be 'warming up', but they got lost, somehow, somewhere in the gentle press of Freddie's mouth against mine.

I'd had dreams like this. Before I'd even spoken to Freddie. Before I'd ever had a boyfriend or knew what kissing was really like, I'd imagined finding out with Freddie Alton. But the trouble with dreams coming true is, sometimes you find out that they aren't really what you want any more.

Because I had a boyfriend now. And I suddenly knew for absolute certain that the only person in the whole world I really wanted to kiss was him. More than anything. Definitely more than I wanted to kiss Freddie, who I really, really liked, but in a weird kind of way, where I'd stopped wanting to press our mouths together and just wanted to hang out and chat instead.

I put my hand against his chest and pushed.

It wasn't enough to push him *away*, not properly. But it made him step back, quickly, and look down at my hand. He looked a little bit sad when he lifted his head again, but sort of like he'd expected it too.

'Sorry,' he said. 'I just had to know.'

I shook my head. 'It's all right – I think I had to know too. I'd been wondering about it all week. And I like you – I like you so much. But—'

'But you have a boyfriend,' Freddie filled in.

'Yeah. I mean, I hope I do. I spent a whole day ignoring him for stupid reasons yesterday, so I'm not really sure any more. But I still *want* to have a boyfriend, if he hasn't totally gone off me and left to join some sort of retreat for single dancers who've finished with their idiot boyfriends and plan to devote the rest of their lives to their *love of dance* instead.'

I was trying to picture what sort of robes dance monks would wear, when I realized I might have been rambling a bit. Freddie looked slightly confused.

I reached for my point and tried again. 'What I mean is, I can't kiss someone else when I still want to kiss him. It wouldn't be fair.'

Freddie smiled. 'That makes sense. Or I think it does – I'm not sure about the dance retreat bit in the middle.'

'This won't make things weird, will it?' I asked.

'No weirder than you are already.' Freddie laughed. 'But that's what I like about you, so – no.'

He checked his watch and took a couple more steps down the hall. 'We'd better get back, they'll be letting the crowd in soon. Mum's booked three extra seats for her banner.'

I shook my head, grinning and falling into step next to him. 'The only reason I haven't told Dad I'm a reserve yet is that I didn't want to give him time to come up with a supportive chant rhyming with the word *bench*.'

'Clench?' Freddie suggested. 'Wrench?'

'Oh god, don't you start too . . .'

He looked me over and suggested as seriously as he could, 'Hench?'

Laughing, I pushed him through the changing-room doors and out on to the pitch, just in time to see Lacey Laine make her entrance.

THIRTY-EIGHT

There was no other way of describing it: Lacey was wearing the pitch. Her short green dress was covered in the same sort of AstroTurf we were running on, or a designer version that looked exactly like it. She was holding a black and white polka-dot spherical bag and there was something pinned across her face that looked like . . . a net? It was tucked into her hair with little white sticks.

'She's wearing a goal as a veil,' Leroy whispered, sounding awed.

Chidi shook his head. 'That woman knows how to work a look.'

She really, really did. I was distracted for a moment thinking about my future as a POD and wondering what *I* would do to show my support if Leo were starring in a ballet or something. Maybe I could get a jacket made out of red velvet curtains.

But I wasn't distracted enough not to notice that one of Lacey's most important accessories was missing: Kayla wasn't with her.

I jogged back to the dugout where I'd left my phone

and sent her a quick message.

> **Where are you? Need you here to stop Dad rage-rushing the pitch when he sees I'm not on.**

And then another.

> **Worried about you too, I suppose. A bit.**

If I'd been honest about it, I'd have said I was considering ditching the match altogether to go and look for her. They'd have to get a *reserve* reserve. It's not like I'd be able to focus on the game without knowing where she was.

Just as I was about to put it away, my phone buzzed in my hand. I'd been sent a video.

A video of someone's feet.

Someone's feet in jazz shoes, with baggy black dance trousers draping over the top of them. Slowly, the owner of the feet pointed one toe out in front of him, and a gentle voice started to narrate.

'*I've realized there are a lot of similarities between football and dance,*' the voice said. On-screen, the feet pointed out and pushed upward in one delicate motion.

'*We both have to stay on our toes . . .*'

The video panned out, and someone turned the

camera round so it focused on a mirror opposite, showing their body from the neck down. He did a little dip, then kicked upwards, his foot easily reaching his chest. And then launched into the most graceful can-can I'd ever seen. *Definitely* more impressive than the version I'd seen Aunt Julie do on the dance floor at her wedding, right before she put a heel through the back of her dress and fell into the cake.

The dance kept up for a few seconds before the camera panned up, bringing Leo's face into shot. I smiled. It was just my automatic response to him now.

'*And we both have to keep on kicking. Glad to know you still are – I was worried for a minute yesterday. Anyway, I just wanted to say good luck properly. From my feet to yours. Miss you, Dyl. See you later.*'

I couldn't wait. I was going to video call him the first spare second I had.

But I still hadn't heard from Kayla, and my spare seconds were running out fast.

Jez had come over from working with 'his' team of pros, like he'd only just remembered we existed. He called everyone into a huddle. Even reserves were included in the team talk, but I took my time getting over there so I wouldn't have to stand too close.

'Now,' Jez was saying, 'remember, not only are your folks going to be out there today, but also some people who *really* matter. People who'll be eyeing you up, wondering if you're worth anything. And most of you lot are pushing it for getting into a youth squad, so if you're not worth anything now, you never will be. Remember that. After today, you may as well forget it. So get on the pitch and just try not to make total embarrassments of yourselves.'

He stood up, dusting his hands off like he'd just finished a satisfying day's work. The rest of us stood there silently, not quite sure what to make of his pep talk. Not quite sure it had even been one.

Chidi looked like he wanted to puke with nerves. Leroy looked like he might wet himself and then puke after.

'Go on then – wait in the changing room till you're called out.' A smirk curling across his face, Jez turned and walked away.

Our team headed slowly off the pitch, totally disheartened.

In the changing rooms people threw themselves onto benches or slumped against the wall. It looked like we'd been defeated already. Only Freddie stayed standing, crossing his arms over his chest so tightly, I was concerned he might snap himself in half.

He did snap, but not like that.

'What *are* footballer players actually worth?' he barked out finally.

'United's last signing was twelve point three million,' Laurie replied sullenly.

'Right, but that's just what they're worth to a club. For a few years, until they get injured or until someone decides they don't live up to that figure any more. And it's a stupid amount, anyway. Twelve million? You could equip a hospital with that kind of money, save lives. Who decides a footballer's worth more than that? And how many players even make that kind of money, out of the hundreds of thousands who want to? That's not *worth*; that's just money. So what are footballer players actually worth? What's *football* worth?'

No one answered. Even I'd developed paralysis of the vocal chords again, for the first time since Freddie and me had become friends. But I'd decided I wasn't going to do that any more. I wasn't going to freeze up just because I didn't feel good enough.

'It's worth something,' I said finally. Even if I sounded like Miss Piggy's younger sister, at least I was speaking. 'It's worth a lot for the look my dad gets on his face when his team wins. Or for the time me and my brother share watching the highlights. It's worth it if you love it. But *love*'s the valuable bit. It's pointless if you're spending the whole time wondering if you're good enough. It's not *us* who have to be worth it – it's the game.'

Freddie was watching me. He had that intent look from before, intent enough that I figured out an escape route just in case he wanted to swing across the room on his kitbag and kiss me again. I didn't think that was what it was about, though.

'Yeah.' Chidi was nodding. 'Yeah, it's only worth it if we're loving it, and I've got to say, I'm *not* loving it with Jez as our coach.'

There was a murmur of agreement.

'So we ditch him,' I said, feeling a thrill of rebellion. 'He's not with our team any more, anyway, so he can't be our coach. And who are the opposition? A load of players who've been told they aren't worth what they used to be.'

'Feet of the Future versus Feet of the Past?' Chidi laughed.

'It's a shame it's too late to get *that* put on a banner,' Freddie said. 'OK, so let's go out and see whether they can make this game worth it to us.'

Noise was starting to creep in from the pitch. 'Can we watch the cheerleaders first?' Aaron called from where he'd been peering out of the door. 'They're doing that Dead Drop routine.'

I knew they'd been practising it – that was why they were able to pull it off so quickly with us the other night. It would be cool to see it done when I didn't have to be

257

scared of something going wrong. 'I think we could all use a bit of cheer.'

I walked over to help Aaron hold the doors open so everyone could see, just as the cheer squad threw their smallest member high, high up into the air.

And the whole crowd gasped as Kayla, in a cheer uniform with a little flippy skirt, spun towards the ground and vanished out of sight.

THIRTY-NINE

It was *so* unfair. Kayla had joined the cheer squad on the very last day of the camp, and now she was performing in front of everyone as if she'd been there all the time. Now *I'd* look like the only one who'd been keeping secrets from Mum and Dad.

She shook her pom-poms at me triumphantly as the cheerleaders flounced off the pitch, and I only smiled incredibly proudly for a *second*. That would teach her.

I hoped Mum had managed to snap a few pictures for Kayla to send to her dad.

As we walked on, and the crowd started to make some noise, I tipped my head up and scanned the stands, trying to spot my parents.

I noticed Freddie's mum first. It wasn't hard – she and his dad were sitting in the front row between two giant cardboard cut-outs of trophies with Freddie's name on, while holding up a banner reading, *FREDDIE ALTON: TOWERS OVER THE REST.*

When I looked a bit closer, I realized they were holding it up in front of the people sitting behind them.

And when someone leaned forward and draped their

own banner over the top of the one the Altons had, I realized who it was.

The new banner read: *FOR DYL KERSHAW, WE'LL ALWAYS ROOT, EVEN IF HE'S A SUBSTITUTE.*

My heart started beating so fast, it might as well have been vibrating. Was that a weird coincidence, or did they know? *How* did they know? And why didn't anyone tell *me*?

Quickly the lower banner was pulled down and put up on top of Dad's one again. Then, moments later, my name was back on display, Dad's banner blocking theirs. It looked like this battle had been going on for a while.

Then, someone in green clicked her way through the terraces towards them. I couldn't quite make out Lacey Laine's Hollywood smile from this distance, but I could tell she was using it to its full effect.

As if they'd been hypnotized into not making a fuss, two people sitting next to the Altons in the front got up and traded places with Mum and Dad. Before long, both banners were held up beside each other. I looked round to find Freddie and smiled the smile of someone dying on the inside.

'After rocket science, do you think she could sort out world peace? Anyway, at least we've found the cringe section of the stadium. Do you think we can spend the whole match not looking over there?'

'I think we can try . . .' Freddie paused and frowned. 'Is that *music*?'

It sounded like it. I looked up at the speakers, wondering if someone had left the cheer squad's tracks running. Only it didn't sound like the kind of upbeat pop they did their routines to.

It was a deep, melodic blast, like a human trumpet blare. After a minute, I thought I could make out what they were singing.

It was, '*Fauntlerooooooy.*'

'Oh my days – over there.' Chidi sprinted past us, pointing frantically. 'Someone's brought a cult!'

I turned to see where he was pointing. One whole section of the stands was filling up with men in suits and bow ties, all singing. In the middle at the front, wearing a dress with a red dragon emblazoned across it, was the woman I'd seen staring at me from a car last night.

Leroy's mum.

'No,' I said. 'She's brought an entire Welsh male voice choir.'

As more of them took their seats, the song became so loud and booming, it drowned out all other noise in the stadium. '*Fauntleroy, he's our boy. Fauntleroy, he's our booooy . . .*'

Now I understood why my telling Leroy no one would know if he was a bad captain hadn't cheered him up. His mum must have bussed in the whole village. I looked around for where he was cowering now, only to find him standing right in the middle of us, beaming. He might have swollen to twice his size with pride. The nerves seemed to have evaporated in the warmth of the music.

He noticed me and sighed happily. 'Ah, there's nothing like home comforts, is there.'

Across on the other stand, even Dad and Freddie's mum had let their banners sink to the ground, accepting defeat in the battle of the superfans. They'd be up and waving again soon, I knew, but I couldn't really make myself mind.

Dad *knew* I'd been made a substitute, and all he'd done differently had been to make up a new rhyme. That was better support than a thousand banners held by a thousand choristers could ever be.

I couldn't help singing along to the Fauntleroy song myself as I went to take my place on the bench.

Scowling, Jez stamped his way towards the centre circle to meet Leroy for a coin toss that would determine who'd pick the direction of play. A second later, Leroy punched the air and turned to nod to the rest of the team that we'd get to play the way we'd been training. The choir let out a joyful blast. It was a small point in our favour.

Then the whistle blew, and the game was under way.

Jez had told us beforehand what formation we'd be playing. Football's a bit like chess, in that the players are like pieces, and part of the strategy involves positioning them in the right spots to move about on the pitch. Whether your team's stronger in attack or defence, you can find a formation that plays to your strengths – or takes advantage of the opposite team's weak points.

Jez had given us a defensive structure, and that made me suspicious. After all, we had youth on our side, which meant faster legs, and even if Laurie Deering wasn't a great person, he was a pretty great striker. Plus Freddie and Leroy were quick in the midfield, and Chidi ran so fast, you couldn't see his legs moving – a perfect sweeper.

The pros would have the skill to get around our defences. We had to attack. That's what Leroy had messaged me to say earlier, and I'd agreed. It's what he told everyone else right before they went out too. So the team lined up in one of the most aggressive formations in football. The one the big teams use when they're out to destroy: 4 – 3 – 3. Definitely not what Jez had picked out for us.

Across the field, our coach's face was turning so red, he could have been mistaken for a stop sign, with a white line of gritted teeth across the middle.

But there wasn't any stopping us now.

FORTY

By the second half, after the team had come off to fuel up with energy drinks and power bars, and after Jez had completely ignored us to work with the pro team instead, we were playing at a drawn score of one goal to each side.

Ending the match with a score of one all with a group of students wasn't going to cut it for Jez, though. I watched him stalk smugly back on to the pitch and wondered exactly what strategy he thought he'd come up with to secure victory.

Our own tactic was pretty simple: get the ball to Laurie. Freddie was the other option, but Laurie had scored our first goal, and he was our best shot at victory, in more ways than one. We'd have a couple of defenders marking the pro's best strikers, but no matter how quick we were, they always seemed to find a way to dodge out at the right moment. So what we had to do was get the ball to Laurie – and get it there fast.

So far, it was *nearly* working. We'd kept the ball in our own half more of the match than not, which was impressive on its own. But it seemed like there was always someone waiting to snatch it away before anyone got a chance at goal.

Watching from a distance, I could see the opportunities when they opened up, and it was making me itch to rush out there and take advantage. I had my hands hooked under the side of the bench just to keep me there.

Up in the crowd, I could see Dad had pulled out a new banner. This one said: *SUB ON DYLAN, YOU KNOW YOU SHOULD. THE OTHER PLAYERS ARE FINE, BUT HE'S MUCH MORE GOOD.*

Dad's rhymes didn't get better when he wrote them in a rush. Anyway, he really needn't have bothered. With about fifteen minutes left on the clock, nobody was coming off to let me sub for them. It would take a coach to decide that, and ours was playing viciously for the opposing team.

The Altons were still waving their banner. With the choir having hushed to concentrate on the game, I could hear Freddie's mum screaming his name.

And next to them, there was a banner that I was sure hadn't been there before. Printed on what looked like a leopard-print scarf, it read simply: *GO, STUDENTS!*

It was being waved furiously by Lacey Laine.

I was so busy watching the crowd, I almost missed what was happening on the field. But suddenly everyone was on their feet, yelling at twice the volume, and I turned my head to see Laurie Deering making an urgent dash up the pitch. This was the best chance he'd had all match: he was practically unmarked, except for one of the pro team gradually catching him up.

At the last second, the pro player overtook Laurie, and I saw him look up and hesitate. The name on the back of the pro's shirt read: *DUTTON*.

I held my breath as Laurie's confidence flickered for a second, but then he drew his leg back to take the chance at goal . . . just as Jez slid in and kicked the other leg out from under him.

It was a clear foul; there was no mistaking it. Jez immediately started yelling that he'd been going for the ball, but there was going to be a boot-shaped bruise on Laurie's shin tomorrow. The fall had sent him down at a really odd angle, and he lay motionless on the pitch while the medics were called out.

I felt guilt twist up my insides. Laurie had been the hardest to convince to go against Jez's tactics. He'd only agreed because the chance to impress the scouts meant more to him. But now he was the one being made to pay for the choice.

Out on the pitch, everyone went quiet while the medics got Laurie to his feet to see if he could walk. He took a couple of wobbly steps forward and shook his head, holding out his arms for support to get over to the bench.

The bench.

I don't know why it didn't click right away. Maybe because Freddie had started miming some weird kind of strip routine in the background, and – even if he was just a friend – it was a bit distracting. But it took me longer than it should to figure out he was miming for me to take off the jumper I'd put on to keep warm and start warming up properly. I was going to be playing after all.

I did some quick stretches and jogged on to the pitch, where Jez had somehow talked himself out of a red card for an obvious foul by telling the referee that he'd never intentionally tackle one of his own students. It was total nonsense – one of his favourite things was showing us how good he was at swiping the ball from someone else – but apparently he was being believed this time.

I looked at Freddie, then up at the stands. Our parents would be staging a pitch invasion if Jez wasn't careful. Dad had form. When I got fouled in a junior school match, I came off to find him declaring a thumb war with the eight-year-old who'd tripped me.

'Focus,' Freddie said softly. 'They're not there. It's just you and the ball.'

'Easier said than done.'

I'd seen Dad change banners when I'd looked across.

The new one was just a picture of me next to the line: *THAT'S MY SON!*

Fifteen minutes. I had that long to not let him down.

The ref blew his whistle, and they passed in a blur.

It felt like we were doing well, but it's never as easy to find the chances to score when you're playing the game as it is when you're watching. Somehow, every time I turned to pass the ball to Freddie or Leroy, or to see if Chidi could get it closer to goal, there was a pro player blocking me. All we were managing to do was drift from one side of the pitch to the other, and back again. Over and over. The crowd must have thought they were watching a tennis match.

Then the fifteen minutes were gone, and we were into a final six of extra time, added on because of Laurie's injury. After that, we'd be into penalties, and one of our best strikers was already down.

Three minutes in, Chidi passed the ball my way, and for the first time I saw clear green space ahead. I ran for it. Jez ducked in ahead of me, a constant, malevolent presence, like one of those wasps that won't leave you alone at a picnic.

I passed to Freddie. Jez dropped back as another player loomed up on Freddie's right. I kept running, unmarked while I didn't have the ball.

Freddie passed back.

I was so close. I could see the open mouth of the goal. I could see their keeper locking eyes with me. Already, he was beginning the game of figuring out which way I'd go.

I turned, aiming my body the way I'd aim my kick – and Jez's shadow fell across the grass in front of me. Things were moving at warp speed. Jez crowded in towards me, blocking any chance I had at goal, and I . . .

Passed sideways.

The ball flew across to Leroy, who was right in front of the goal. An unthreatening presence for most of the match, he didn't have anyone on his tail.

It was so quick that the keeper was still looking at me as Leroy's goal went in. And the whistle blew to end the match.

The crowd was deafening. Every single mum, dad and all the strangers who'd picked up a free ticket to see some former glories playing one more time joined in with the new chorus of *'Fauntleroy, he's our boy'* ringing out around them.

Leroy pulled his shirt over his head and threw it in the air, whooping, 'I told you I'm good under pressure!'

And Jez fell over.

Or he didn't fall over, exactly. He tripped. I'd seen the loose lace trailing from his boot after he'd aimed that kick at Laurie. When he'd skidded back, confused by my sudden change of direction, it caught on the spikes of the opposite boot.

He literally tripped over his own feet and sailed over backwards, smacking his head against the AstroTurf.

'What happened?' he asked groggily, as the medics jogged towards him.

Freddie came up and threw an arm round my shoulder, looking down at where Jez lay. 'I think you fouled yourself.'

I pulled a face. 'I hope that's only in one sense of the word.'

Freddie laughed, and I pulled him with me to join the rest of the team celebrating by leaping and spinning round in front of the goal. Leroy was doing the robot. Leo had been right. There isn't that much difference between football and dancing at all.

FORTY-ONE

'I can't *believe* you didn't tell us how awful that man was.' Mum's knuckles were turning white around the handles of her handbag as we walked through the hotel lobby to the dining room where the trophy ceremony was going to be held. If Jez didn't keep out of her way, I could see her smacking him with it.

'I can't believe you didn't tell me you *knew* I'd been left on the bench,' I protested. 'How long were you keeping that a secret?'

'How long were *you*?' Dad replied drily.

I hated it when he had a good point.

'We called yesterday to ask what position you'd be playing,' Mum said. 'Because you'd told us the team wouldn't be told in advance, we exercised our parental rights to obtain additional information.'

'I wanted to make sure I had a rhyme,' Dad added helpfully.

'Well, you managed that, at least. And hey, at least *one* of your sons is a future star athlete.' Jude had slain the opposition at his demonstration match. They didn't give trophies out to five-year-olds, but he was wearing his

I PARTICIPATED rosette with as much pride as he would a gold medal.

'They're campaigning to make football the first powerchair sport in the Paralympics,' Dad said proudly. 'I reckon I've got a contender for England captain here.'

Jude tipped his head back to beam up at us. 'I precipitated!'

I grinned in return. 'Yeah, I heard you were the best precipitator in the place.'

'But,' Dad said, reaching out to ruffle Jude's hair, 'I don't know what you think there is to be ashamed about, being a sub. You're a vital part of the team on that bench.'

'What sort of vital part?' I asked. 'The third wheel? I only got to play because Laurie was hurt.'

'And you showed more class in those final minutes than anyone on the pitch. The game would fall apart without reserves, Dylan. A good coach picks his subs as carefully as he picks his first team. You bring a sub on when your opposition are starting to get tired legs, and they'll be uncatchable. Or if one of the players is having a bad day – bring on a reserve who isn't. They can completely change a game. You should know that, after today.'

When I thought about it, what Dad was saying was a nicer version of the dressing-down Jez had given me the other day. The one I thought I'd learned my lesson from. It seemed like I might need to hear it a few more times. 'It's not about how good the player is; it's about how good they make the team.'

'That's my boy.' Dad winked. Then he shrugged and went on, 'But you should have started in a forward spot. The man must be coaching blindfold to have missed that.'

Jez hadn't missed anything. That was exactly why he didn't want me to play. But I'd told Mum and Dad enough about how rubbish Jez was as a coach already. The match was over, and us winning had given Jez all the payback he deserved.

Walking next to Jude reminded me to keep an eye out for any sign of the Ratbusters, but it looked like they'd been told to keep out of sight during the celebration. There was a different vehicle pulled up by the doors, though. I nudged Kayla.

'If we duck out of this party, maybe we can stow away in there?'

The Deathsplash tour bus was standing with its storage section open, a collection of black and silver boxes and interesting-looking wires just inside.

Kayla sighed. 'I've made my peace with missing the concert. Deathsplash and I may be star-crossed music lovers when it comes to me seeing them perform live, but we'll always have breakfast, hot dogs and hamsters.'

I slung an arm round her shoulders. 'And at least you won't have to lie to your dad about where you are tonight. Trust me, that never works out.'

'Yes – heaven forbid I keep secrets. I might turn out like you.' Kayla smiled.

'Like I said, more people have been keeping secrets *from* me. Like Leo – did you know this big show he's been rehearsing for was tonight? Because he only mentioned it to me when I tried to call just now.'

Kayla shook her head. 'I didn't know anything about it.'

'Big show?' Dad asked, clearing his throat. 'Didn't mention what it was, did he?'

'No.' I sighed, like that mattered. 'It could be anything from *Swan Lake* to *Escalators: A Steps Tribute Performance* for all I know. That isn't the point. The point is, if I'd known, maybe we could have skipped the party and gone back home tonight. At least I'd have got to see him for a couple of days.' I let a little bit of a whine creep into my voice. It had been a stressful few days; surely I deserved *something* going right for a change.

'We're here for the weekend,' Dad said firmly. 'I've booked us tickets for a falconry display tomorrow.'

Oh, no. 'Last time we went to one of those, you beat all the little kids to being chosen to participate, and then

275

you *lost the bird.*' I whimpered, physically pained by the memory of all those crying children when Dad joked it had probably been eaten by a cat. 'It's going to be a *nightmare.*'

'Tough,' Dad said. 'It's going to be a nightmare we have as a *family.*'

He really knew how to make it sound appealing.

Before I could come up with a new protest, or consult Kayla for my legal rights in making an official appeal against cruel and unjust treatment, I spotted Freddie hovering just outside the doors of the dining room.

Like me and Kayla, he'd decided to dress up this evening. Except, where my suit was left over from my uncle's wedding last year, and I'd grown at least three inches since then – which was exactly how much ankle the trousers exposed – Freddie's looked like it had been hand sewn by a fancy tailor first thing that morning. My jacket, in opposition to my trousers, was three sizes too big, as Mum still insisted on buying me things to 'grow into', despite the fact I'd just turned fifteen, and my shoulders probably weren't going to pop out to the size of a pro-bodybuilder's overnight.

Freddie looked like he'd just fallen out of the pages of one of those bridal magazines I've definitely never picked up and flicked through in the dentist's office.

He looked amazing. And I *still* only wanted him to be my friend.

Kayla skipped forward and caught one of Freddie's hands. She looked well matched with him, wearing a short, dark navy dress with a skirt that faded out into pale pink at the hem. It glittered with tiny sequin stars – the dress she should have been wearing for the concert later. 'What are you lurking out here for? Shouldn't you be helping your mum with any last-minute decorating?'

'Oh, she's finished it.' Freddie grinned. 'It's a load of balls.'

Mum's eyebrows curved into two exclamation marks. 'I'm not sure that's appropriate language in front of the children.'

I thought she might have meant Jude, but she turned and gestured directly at me instead.

'No, no. I mean, literally.' Freddie held open the doors for us, waving an arm at the décor. 'Take a look.'

It was a *load of balls.*

FORTY-TWO

No one could say Freddie's mum didn't know how to work a theme. Footballs of every shape and size filled the room – strung above the tables like bunting, tied together into a makeshift chandelier – there were even miniature footballs on sticks poking out between floral arrangements on the table. It looked like a weirdly formal version of one of the rooms at Jude's soft-play centre.

We must have been among the last to arrive. The tables were filling up fast with other team members and their families. Even some of the pros had turned up, along with a photographer from the local paper who was lurking around a table at one end of the room, where a huge trophy took pride of place.

'It's not real,' Freddie said, catching me looking. 'Mum bought a plastic Tudor goblet from a party shop in the Arndale Centre and "distressed it". She nearly knocked Dad out with the paint fumes.'

My dad had dashed up to take a selfie with it anyway. He looked around the room with the same awed expression Jude had worn last Christmas, when he assumed every present under the tree was meant for him. If Mum didn't put her foot down fast, I could tell he'd have plans for redecorating when we got home.

Freddie's mum popped up next to Dad, beaming proudly, and took his camera to take a better photo. Then they got one together, thumbs up next to the plastic cup.

I nudged Freddie. 'It's like one of those films where the supervillains team up. They're going to be unstoppable now.'

Freddie groaned. 'I'm pretty sure Mum's been looking up the cost of hiring her own choir already.'

'Speaking of which,' Kayla cut in, 'it looks like Flauntyboy arrived early to make sure no one was having too much fun.'

Leroy and his mum were sitting together on the opposite side of the room. It didn't look like they'd brought any musical accompaniment with them this time.

I frowned at Kayla. 'Isn't it about time you stopped pretending you don't know his name? He was great today, and he's been helping you all week. Just because you've met the only person on earth who takes rules more seriously than you do.'

'Only the stupid ones!' Kayla retorted, before sighing huffily. 'Fine. I was just going to suggest we join *Leroy's* table before someone else does, anyway.'

'Oh . . .' I raised my eyebrows. 'Good idea.'

Freddie went to sit with his family, while mine packed round the table with Leroy and Mrs Hughes, Dad making both of them blush the exact same colour by clapping Leroy on the back and calling him a 'top skipper'.

We'd just taken our seats when the lights dimmed, and Jez and Lacey made their entrance.

Jez had changed out of his kit from earlier, and he had a plaster over the back of his head, but he was still wearing the same pained expression: teeth gritted tightly together like he'd just sat on a beehive and was trying not to let anyone know. He managed to arrange his mouth into an upward curve that would *almost* have resembled a smile had it not seemed so much like he was ready to bite anyone who got too close.

So Lacey was brave to be walking at his side. I noticed they weren't arm in arm, but, judging from the gasps round the room, no one else was paying attention to anything except her dress. Dresses might not be my thing, but even I had to admit this one was pretty spectacular. She looked like she'd stepped out of the final scene of a Disney film, one of the ones where the princess *does* go to the ball. Her golden skirt was as wide as she was tall and made of netting with what looked like fairy lights woven into it: she literally glowed. Even in an expensive suit, Jez looked drab in comparison.

'That's it – I'm googling *tailor electricians* immediately,' Kayla whispered. 'That's *unbelievable*.'

'Yes,' Leroy agreed, much too loudly. 'A high-visibility vest would be cheaper and much more efficient. I hope she's not planning to plug it into the mains.'

Kayla rolled her eyes at me, obviously being very restrained about not thumping her head against the table. She snapped a quick photo of Lacey's dress and pulled out her phone – I could already guess she was about to text her dad with the first item on her Christmas list for this year.

As Jez and Lacey took up their places on either side of the trophy table, I could see Jez look down and briefly scan the menu. I'd checked it earlier, and I bit my lip not to smile now as he read that we were about to be served our choice of Jez Jalfrezi or Dutton Mutton Dhansak. That's the problem with bad curries: they repeat on you for *ages*.

Narrowing his eyes, he reached to snap up a glass from the table, picking up a spoon to tap it with – as if all the attention in the room wasn't already on him. By now, most of the parents must have started to hear rumours about his coaching style.

'Right,' Jez started, clearly settling in for a lengthy speech.

I didn't mind – our team had completely showed him up today, and he was finally going to have to admit it. He could take all the time in the world.

'Nice to see all these faces one last time,' Jez said, clearly making it sound like it was seeing us for the *last time* that was the good bit. 'Today was a roller coaster of a match. We had ups, we had downs, and half you lads looked like you were going to wet yourselves with nerves before the ride started. But I think you knew I was looking out for you all along. See, the thing with football is, it's not always about being good – it's about *thinking* you're good.'

Except, we had been good – *really* good.

Kayla kicked me under the table, pulling a confused face. I shook my head, waiting to see where this was going.

'And that's my job, as coach. To let you lot think you're good. So if we went a bit easy on you today, it's worth it to see the boost it gave you. Of course, you can't always expect people to let you win . . .'

A murmur went up from where Chidi's family were sitting. And Freddie's.

Let us win?

Jez went on as if he couldn't hear. 'But you can always remember this one time you did.' He scooped up the trophy on the table and held it high. 'So I'm accepting this one for all of you. We deserve it.'

Across the room, Laurie Deering stood up, leaning heavily on a brand-new crutch. 'You don't deserve anything.'

'Except a clip round the ear,' Mrs Hughes said fiercely.

'Leroy earned that cup.' Freddie put his hands on the table and stood up too.

Leroy joined them. 'We all did!'

'Fluffy!' yelled Jude, waving his hands in the air.

'I know you like to be included, but that's a bit of a tangent,' I said to him, while Dad and Mrs Alton pushed back their seats and started marching up to the top table.

The families of the rest of the team were crowding in behind them. I could hear snatches of complaints like fouled a child and how can a coach play against his own team and just in it for himself.

But Jude was still waving and yelping, 'No, it's Fluffy! I found him! He's there – He's there!'

I looked up to where he was gesturing. Swaying above Jez Dutton's head, as he tried to keep it out of the grip of a dozen angry football families, there was a small hamster peering out of a large gold trophy.

'Wait—' I started, diving under the table to try and get through the crowd.

Kayla moved at the same time as me, climbing over the rows of chairs. 'Stop! Don't let him drop the—'

But we were too late.

Neither of us reached Jez in time to stop him tilting the trophy a little too far . . . pouring its orange, fuzzy contents straight on to his own head.

FORTY-THREE

'A RAT! A RAT! GET IT OFF ME!' Jez was screaming.

For some reason, he'd clambered on to a chair, even though Fluffy was already on him, trying to pick his way through spikes of gelled hair.

'He's not a *rat* – he's a *HAMSTER!*' I could hear Jude yelling from the back of the room.

'Get Fluffy!' Kayla yelled at me, climbing on to one of the tables as I emerged out from under a black and white tablecloth.

A waiter tried to get in between me and Jez's table, but I skirted round him. 'We have to save that hamster!'

Meanwhile, Jez was doing his best to send Fluffy flying, reeling round on the chair with his arms whirling. I kept one eye on Kayla as we coordinated our rescue attempt. I flung my arms round Jez's waist, keeping his flailing limbs pinned to his sides while Kayla tried to climb up beside him.

Rearing back, Jez's shadow was caught by the light of the football chandelier, projecting the massive black silhouette of a monstrous hamster on to the opposite wall. Jez yelped in fear and swept a hand towards his own scalp, as if he were swatting a giant fly.

'Fluffy, no!'

My yell got lost in a chorus of screams as all the lights in the room suddenly went out.

I thought I felt something small and furry skitter across my shoulders and skim down my shirt to the floor.

The room was in chaos. All around me, I could hear the sound of glasses tipping, plates sliding to the floor, and tables creaking as people tripped over carefully placed footballs and fell into each other. Everyone was scrabbling around in the pitch-black – until a ghostly, glowing figure swept across to take my hand.

'This way – I think I saw him!' Lacey Laine exclaimed.

With Kayla, Leroy and Freddie following in the trail of her light-up skirt, we ran for the door.

The lights flickered and came back on, dimmer than they were before.

'What was that?' Mrs Hughes was saying anxiously. 'Does anyone smell smoke?'

Mum was standing in the middle of the room, one hand resting soothingly on Jude's head, the other caught in Dad's collar, keeping him from knocking Jez off his chair. She looked up in wonder. '*Mary the maid!*'

'It doesn't matter – there he goes!' Kayla pointed to the doors that led back to the lobby as Fluffy skittered through.

From just outside, I could hear Alfie the porter screaming, 'Rat! The rat came back!'

'How many bright orange rats have these people seen?' I asked, as I bolted towards the doors, with Kayla, Lacey, Freddie and Leroy close behind.

'Where did he go? The hamst – Rat. Where did the rat go?' Kayla asked Alfie, while we spread out to cover as much ground as possible.

Ms Toshkhani was on the phone behind the desk, probably summoning the Ratbusters to get down there as fast as possible.

Alfie pointed towards the car-park doors.

I gasped. 'No, no – he can't have gone out there.' The Deathsplash tour bus was revving its engines as I spoke. 'He'll be flattened! I'm not bringing my little brother back a hamster he can use as a coaster.'

'We have to go and see.' Kayla hooked her arm in mine and dragged me to the door.

The Deathsplash groupies had finally all abandoned the hotel – they were probably already at Old Trafford, getting ready to watch the concert. One of their roadies strolled past us as we scanned the tarmac.

'Kayla?' Leroy said, coming outside to join us.

'If you're about to tell me it's against the rules to leave the venue during an event, I'll scream,' she snapped.

'No,' he said, sounding a little stung. 'But – is that the hamster you've been looking for?'

He pointed to the doors of the bus, which were just sliding closed behind the roadie . . . the roadie and the slightly open guitar case in his arms, through which an orange, whiskery face was only just visible.

Fluffy.

'Stop that bus!' Kayla and I both surged forward as one, and I was *sure* I saw the driver look over at us and roll his eyes, before turning the black, glittering bus out of the hotel grounds and off into the night.

It was over.

Fluffy was off to live a rock-and-roll lifestyle, and Kayla and I didn't even have tickets to watch. We stood, panting breathlessly, in the middle of the car park.

'What do we do now?' I asked her, staring after the bus.

She just shook her head.

'Road trip?' someone asked brightly. Lacey and her illuminated dress stepped forward and took both our hands. 'How does a visit to Old Trafford sound?'

'But –' I stared at her.

'We –' Kayla shook her head. 'We've been trying to get tickets all week. There's no way they'll let us in for a hamster.'

'Oh, maybe not the normal way.' Lacey grinned at us

as if we were both just a little bit dopey. 'We'll just have to go in backstage.'

Kayla turned so pale so suddenly that I reached a hand out to catch her arm before I managed to say, 'Yes! Please? Can we?'

'No,' said Jez Dutton.

All five of us spun round to see Jez leaning against the lobby doors. Now the hamster was safely off the premises, he seemed to have regained his composure.

'*Excuse me?*' Lacey said.

He shook his head. 'I said no, Lace. I forbid you to take those kids out of here. And you're not taking the car. You try it, and you can forget about us.'

Lacey's perfectly pink mouth twisted into a tight knot. 'I think you're forgetting one or two things, *Jeremy*,' she said.

'*Jeremy*,' Freddie mouthed across at me. If there's one thing mums and teachers have in common, it's a way of using your full name when they're really angry. Apparently girlfriends did it too.

'First of all, *I* paid for the car. Second, the whole world's forgotten about you already. Do you really think I'll have that hard a time doing the same?' She twisted a heel on the ground like she was stubbing out a cigarette. 'And third, like I told you last night, you don't get to tell me what to do. Not any more.'

She whipped a phone out of her pocket and pressed a button before speaking into it.

'Teri, bring the car round. We're taking the party somewhere else.'

Jez looked like she'd reached out and slapped him from right across the car park. He was silent for a minute before starting to stumble across towards us. 'Lace? Lace . . . you don't mean that. I didn't mean . . . Lace?'

She held up the palm of her hand – American reality-show sign language for *Please stop talking* – as a black car swung in through the car-park gates.

'Everyone coming?' Lacey asked us chirpily.

Leroy held up his own phone. 'I've been texting Mum. She says she'll tell everyone and follow the car.'

'Well, thank goodness for your quick thinking,' Kayla said, teasing. Though, weirdly, she sounded sort of fond.

I looked up at Lacey as she opened the back door to the car. It would be *so* much easier to just get another orange hamster from the nearest pet shop. But we couldn't abandon Fluffy to a life on the road. He was only little, and rock stars were probably terrible influences. He'd be swallowing too many pellets and wrecking his cage before we knew it.

So I nodded at Lacey. 'Yeah, I'm coming. I guess everyone is.'

FORTY-FOUR

It turns out to be amazingly easy to get backstage at concerts if you're really, really attractive and at least a little bit famous.

Lacey winked at security as we waltzed in through one of the entrances usually reserved for premier-league footballers or rock stars. 'I've got a date with Rick Deathsplash.'

Kayla flicked her aquamarine hair and followed suit. 'And I've got one with Jenna Deathsplash.'

Freddie, Leroy and me were up next.

Leroy smiled coquettishly at the hulking guard. 'And we're here to see . . .' He paused, squinting uncertainly at me. 'Are they a band, these Deathsplashers? Or some sort of comedy act?'

'They're with me,' Lacey interrupted, taking wristband passes for each of us as Kayla dragged Leroy through by one of his sleeves. 'Every girl needs an entourage.'

Backstage was madness. There were men in black running backwards and forwards holding rolls of gaffer tape as thick as car wheels and clutching bundles of wires, or electric guitars, or oversized inflatable props.

As we edged around to the stage area, I could see backing dancers warming up for the show. There was a troupe of vampire girls in red and black tutus, and a motley collection of other spooky creatures behind them: evil clowns doing high kicks, and apparitions in white sheets or black cloaks bending and stretching. There was even a werewolf practising pirouettes, its giant foam head a blur as it spun.

For a moment, it almost made me nostalgic. Although when I'd watched Leo warm up with those kinds of moves, he'd been dressed as a giant orange hamster, not something that might eat hamsters as a midnight snack.

And speaking of hamsters . . .

'We have to track down Fluffy,' I said firmly.

The others were gawping as much as I was, even Lacey looked a little bit awed by the spectacle. But there wasn't much time. In twenty minutes, the band would hit the stage, and we'd probably get penned in somewhere to watch. Our Fluffy-finding minutes were ticking down fast.

'We should find that roadie,' Kayla said, wrenching her eyes away from the stage. 'He had the hamster last.'

'But it was in an instrument case – shouldn't we look for where they stash those first?' Freddie asked.

Lacey swept up her skirt in one hand and looped her other arm through Kayla's. 'If we split up, we can do both. Kayla, Leroy and I can charm a few people into telling us if Fluffy was spotted on the bus. You two, find where they store the instruments.'

She swept off, Kayla and Leroy keeping up on either side. I wasn't sure exactly how *Leroy* was going to help with their charm offensive, even if he could be quite persuasive when he got that kicked-puppy air about him.

There wasn't time to wonder about it for long. We had to find out where the band's instruments were kept, and it wasn't exactly the kind of question we could just ask someone. It was one of those situations where if you didn't know, you probably weren't supposed to. Asking might make it sound like we planned to grab a couple of guitars and storm the stage during the show.

Nobody here was going to know that my stage fright was legendary, or that the only instrument I'd ever learned to play was the recorder – and even then, I'd never got much further than the melodic masterpiece that was 'Gilbert Goblin Gobbled Up Goats'.

Last time I'd tried karaoke, I was pretty sure people had rioted just to get me to stop singing. I definitely wasn't cut out for rock stardom. So we had to think. With Freddie looking blank, I tried to remember anything that might be useful from the thousands of concert videos Kayla had made me watch.

'They get through dozens of guitars during the show,' I said slowly. 'They've even got wooden acoustic ones, just because they look better when they're smashed. Fluffy hid in one of those at the hotel before. His cage is full of wood shavings – it must have felt a bit like a nest.'

'Sounds like a good place to start.' Freddie nodded. 'So if they smash them during the show . . .'

'They have to be kept close to the stage. Really close,' I finished.

We looked at each other and headed towards where the dancers were working through their pre-show warm-ups. Most of the 'backstage' area at the stadium meant the kind of hallways and corridors the players and staff would have used during matches there. But the stage was set up specially, jutting out over the pitch at the Stretford End, with a specially constructed cover over the terraces behind. That was where the preparations were taking place.

As well as the dancers, microphones were being checked, and someone was on their knees taping over wires. Most of the wires led to a big globe-shaped box with an exclamation mark painted on the side and a black and yellow warning: *CAUTION: PYROTECHNICS*.

Freddie and I slid and skidded between the dancers, working on the assumption that if we moved fast and looked like we knew where we were going, nobody would stop us.

We made it into a narrow half-lit room behind the big screens at the back of the stage, where the walls were lined with racks holding an endless line-up of guitars. They were hung individually, each under a label for the band member who'd either play it or destroy it. One row just read *Fakes*.

Another rack in the corner held an almost equal number of empty cases. After taking a deep breath, Freddie headed that way.

'I'll check those.'

I walked towards the fakes wall. 'We're going to get arrested, aren't we? We'll be locked up for unauthorized instrument fondling. I'm sorry I've ended up dragging you into this too.'

Freddie grinned at me, pulling down a case and unzipping it. 'It's not so bad. For a while back there, I thought my night was going to turn out a whole lot worse.'

'Because of everything with Jez?' I asked, peering into the sound hole of one of the decoy guitars, and tipping it upside down to shake out any small, fuzzy stowaways.

'No, because of things with Mum.'

I looked at him. His mum had seemed over the moon, until we totally destroyed her party.

Freddie sighed, scrubbing a hand through the back of his hair as he tugged at another casing. He didn't look at me. 'I sort of came out to her, right before the whole trophy thing happened.'

I wasn't sure exactly when my mouth had fallen open. I pushed a hand up under my chin to close it again. 'You told her you were gay at a *party*?'

It seemed like weird timing, but sometimes you couldn't help where it happened. I'd waited years for the right moment to tell my mum and dad, and I didn't realize until after they found out for themselves that there wasn't any such thing as a wrong moment, really.

But Freddie was shaking his head vigorously. 'No, I haven't told her that yet – although I don't think that's going to be too bad. I mean I told her I didn't want to be a footballer. That I want to be a doctor instead.'

'Oh.' I let out the breath I'd been holding. 'How did that go?'

Freddie grimaced. 'She told me she'd love me no matter what, but didn't I think I might just be going through a phase?'

He shoved another empty case back into the rack, hard, and looked at me. 'I mean, I *love* football – I just can't make myself love it that way.'

I abandoned the latest hamster-free guitar and walked

over to him. 'She'll get used to the idea. It might just take her a while.'

I was reaching out to put a hand on his shoulder, when a dark shadow fell across the floor between us. I looked up to see the dancing werewolf looming menacingly in the doorway.

'It's not what it looks like!' I backed up, hands in the air. 'We weren't doing anything to the guitars. We're . . . We're instrumentologists. This is *research*.'

The werewolf only padded towards us, reaching up to take off his huge hairy head, when we all heard a series of squeals and screeches from just outside. A woman's voice cut in above the rest of the noise. 'Is that a . . . Is that a *rat*?'

Without even looking at each other, Freddie and I bolted for the door, leaving the wolf in our wake.

FORTY-FIVE

We raced out of the backstage room, only to be immediately forced back by the wall of noise that hit us. While we'd been hidden away fondling guitars, someone had decided to let in the crowd.

From our spot behind the stage, we could see the whole stadium. The terraces were filling with Deathsplash fans taking their seats, turning the rows from red to black. The whole place glittered as hundreds of phone screens were lifted up to snap a picture.

And on the platform that had been put up over the pitch, another barrage of fans was rushing towards the stage. Yellow-jacketed security teams linked arms and braced for the onslaught. It was the most terrifying thing I'd ever seen in my life, and I'd once walked in on the staff Christmas party at school, where the deputy head was doing an open-shirted, growly impression of Tom Jones.

This was at least six times scarier than that.

Freddie had kept running, until he realized I wasn't with him any more. He turned back to me, looking confused. 'What's the matter?'

'Oh, nothing. Well, except I can't feel my legs. In fact,

the only bit of me I can feel is my stomach, and that's only because I think I might throw up. Have you *seen all those people*?'

Getting back to my side, Freddie turned to take a look. 'Pretty impressive, isn't it?'

'That's one way of putting it.' I'd definitely have put it another way, but just then it was hard enough work remembering to breathe.

'They can't see us, if it helps. Most of them can't, anyway. There might be a little section right over that side that can see backstage.'

'So just a few thousand people, then.' I tried the usually simple task of putting one foot in front of the other. My legs felt like clay. Clay that was slowly drying and sticking to the floor. If I didn't move soon, I'd probably be stuck there forever, a permanent part of the set.

Just ahead of us, a man wearing a fire-warden vest and a worried expression ran forward. He set a fire extinguisher on the floor a short distance away from the pyrotechnic globe we'd seen being worked on before. Then he edged back and talked into his headset.

'What do you mean, it'll take the technician some time? We haven't *got* time. There's a rodent in the box, and if he chews through the wrong thing, we'll all be seeing sparks.'

Freddie and I looked at each other. I was pretty sure

the look of recognition and horror on his face exactly matched my own.

Fluffy.

Of course the stupid hamster would choose that as a hiding place. It was shaped just like the ball Jude let him run around in at home, only bigger and sturdier. He probably thought he'd been given a luxury upgrade. It was just bad luck that his new penthouse suite happened to be filled with fireworks primed to go off.

I started forward in a rush, as though the rubber bands tying my legs in place had suddenly snapped.

'That's not a rodent – that's our hamster. We have to get him out!' I yelled.

Obviously we had to. The fireworks were probably meant for the moment when Deathsplash rocked on to the stage. I'd heard of singers biting the heads off chickens as part of their act, but I couldn't let Rick Deathsplash start his off by catapulting an innocent hamster into the crowd.

The fire warden held up his hand. 'I don't think so. I have to maintain a five-foot exclusion zone around this equipment until we get technical support. It's been compromised.'

'It's been *nested in*!' I protested, dropping to my knees and starting to crawl towards the globe. Surely it couldn't be too hard to shake Fluffy out of there without both of us going up in a shower of dazzling gold sparks.

My arms and legs moved, but I wasn't getting any further forward. I looked round to find Freddie with a hand twisted in my shirt to hold me back.

'Don't be stupid, Dylan. If Fluffy's chewing through wires in there, it could go off at any second!'

The vampette dancers, who'd been crowding in around us since we'd tracked Fluffy to the explosive globe, started tiptoeing backwards again.

'Then we have to get him out *fast*,' I said, trying to wriggle out of his grip.

And failing.

'Will you let me *go*?'

'I can't let you blow yourself up for a hamster!' Freddie protested.

A white stiletto clicked down on either side of the trail of wires leading to the globe. The fire-safety officer rolled away to one side. Freddie managed to drag me a few feet backwards on the other.

'It's all right, boys,' said Lacey Laine. 'Nobody dies on my watch.'

Leroy and Kayla stood just behind her, Kayla's face lit by the screen of her phone. I could nearly make out the Wikipedia article she was reading, reflected in the gleam of her highlighter.

'According to the serial number, this is a ZF32 golden

strobe mine. It can be operated on a timer and requires a vertical clearance of twenty-five feet for the fireworks' full range.'

'*Twenty-five feet?*' the fire officer squawked, tapping his headset again. 'We're going to need a bigger exclusion zone.'

'No,' Lacey said. 'We're going to need to cut the power.'

'Should we cut the wires?' I asked, still trying to tug myself out of Freddie's hold.

Kayla produced a small make-up bag and drew out some nail scissors. 'It's usually the red one in films. Or is it usually *not* the red one?'

'No – the first thing we need to do is a little simpler than that,' Lacey said. She traced the route of the wiring along its path over the stage to a row of plugs set into the section of rigging that made up the stage wall. Even in her heels, which made her about the same height as me, it was way above her arm's length. She frowned. 'It's the third one along, but I'm not going to be able to reach—'

Before she'd even finished, a hairy shape flung itself at her from the shadows. For a moment, I almost thought Jez had shown up to beg her to come back, but it was the werewolf from before. With an easy kind of grace, he leaped up into the metal rigging and reached out one paw to drag the plug she'd indicated out of its socket.

The lights across the whole of our side of the stage snuffed out.

On the pitch, the noise from the crowd was getting almost unbearable. They must have thought that the lighting change meant the band was about to come on, not that Fluffy hopefully wouldn't be making his stage debut as the Incredible Flying Furball.

I was breathless with nerves. 'Is that it? Does that mean Fluffy's safe?'

Lacey turned on her dress so we could see her again by skirt-light. 'I'm afraid not. It stops the timer, but there's still a chance he could chew on something important inside the ball. The only way to get him out of there's going to mean one of us going in.'

I was going to say that none of us were anywhere near small enough for that, but one more look at the globe let me know what she meant. Where the wires, and Fluffy, had entered the ball, there was an opening just big enough for a human hand.

Shrugging Freddie away, I got to my knees again. 'I'll do it.'

I just couldn't let something terrible happen to Fluffy – not now.

I swallowed down my nerves and tried not to think about the videos we watched in school every November. You should never go back to a lit firework, according to them. They didn't say anything about not picking up a self-detonating hamster, though.

Carefully, I shuffled forward. Reaching the globe, I tilted it very carefully so the opening was clear. Then I stretched out a hand . . .

FORTY-SIX

And found Leroy beside me, grabbing my wrist before I could begin to fish around inside.

'Wait,' he said urgently. 'I think we might be able to lure him out.'

I sat on my heels while he pulled off his backpack and rummaged around in it until, lit by the glow of Lacey's dress, I saw the golden gleam of the trophy Jez had tried to claim for his own.

'How did you get that?' Kayla asked from somewhere over our heads.

'Well, since I'm the captain, I thought it was up to me to take care of it. No one noticed me picking it up once everything kicked off.'

If it wasn't so dark, I'd have thought Leroy was blushing a little.

'So you *stole* it,' I said. 'Who'd have thought.'

Freddie crouched down behind me. 'Do you really think the hamster will want to get back in there? It might have been a traumatic experience the first time.'

'I think he will once he gets a load of these.' From his pocket, Leroy retrieved a handful of carrots from the crudité dishes that had been on tables at the hotel and tipped them into the trophy.

Even in the dark, I think Leroy could feel us staring at him.

'Well, I didn't know how long all that fighting was going to take! I ate a very light lunch.'

'You're a hero, Leroy,' I said. 'All right – let's see if it works.'

I felt at least a little bit safer not having to stick my hand blindly into a box of fireworks and feel around for anything that didn't seem like it was designed to go *bang*. I kept holding the globe in place – moving carefully around it so that if the fireworks were triggered, they wouldn't go off in my face. And Leroy laid the trophy full of treats right by the opening.

We watched in what would have been a hushed silence, if several thousand people just a short distance away hadn't decided to start chanting *Why are we waiting?*

I knew exactly how they felt.

It's amazing how a minute can feel so long when you're waiting to find out if your hamster's about to shower down over Manchester as part of a dazzling light display. After two minutes, I already felt like I couldn't take the agony of it.

'It's no good – I'm going to have to go in after him.'

I started to move back round in front of the globe when Freddie made another grab for me.

'Give it one more minute.'

He caught my arm when he'd meant to get my shoulder. 'Careful, you'll—'

It was too late. The globe slipped from my fingers. It rocked forward, then back towards me.

And tipped out a small, orange hamster, who made straight for the trophy and vanished inside.

Quick as a flash, Kayla dropped her bag over the top to trap him. '*Got you*. Finally! Talk about a hamster being more trouble than it's worth.'

'He only cost about twelve quid from the pet shop,' I said, trying not to pass out with relief, all the nervousness rushing out of me in a sudden flood. 'He's more trouble than a bag of solid-gold bars.'

'Or a room full of exclusive electric guitars,' Freddie put in.

Kayla sighed. 'Or VIP tickets to this concert.'

'Oh, speaking of those,' Leroy said, looking at his phone. 'My mum just texted that she's outside, Dylan. She says you can leave the hamster with her before you go up to your VIP box.'

I raised an eyebrow at him, carefully picking up the trophy while making sure Kayla's bag was tight across the top. 'We don't have a VIP box.'

'Well, Mum says you do. Mum says you've got a box with Kayla and your whole family. And she says not to tell you because it's a huge surprise.'

He finished reading and looked up. 'Oops.'

'But how . . .' Kayla stared at me open-mouthed.

'I don't know!' I hugged the trophy against my chest. 'No one said anything to me.'

Why were my family so *sneaky*?

Kayla looked up at Lacey Laine. 'Did you do this?'

Lacey shook her head. 'Not this time. Besides, I think I'm going to watch the show from back here, just in case they need another little technical assist.'

I don't think Kayla quite believed her, but she ran up for a hug anyway. I sort of wanted to do the same.

'Thanks for everything,' I said, knowing that wasn't nearly enough. 'You saved our hamster. And Kayla's video – and today's game. And turning the power off probably saved me from turning into a human sparkler too.'

She smiled. 'Well, it was hardly rocket science.'

But we all knew she'd have been able to handle that too.

Kayla pulled away with promises to keep in touch and an offer to be Lacey's legal defence if she ever wanted to sue Jez for basically being the worst boyfriend in the world. Though Lacey said as long as he wasn't her boyfriend any more, it didn't really matter.

Then we headed over to the backstage entrance. Kayla was so busy texting her dad that she didn't even notice when she almost walked into someone with wild, dark hair, dressed in a violet sequin bodysuit with a flowing cape.

Alonzo pulled Rick Deathsplash out of her path at the last second. But Rick stopped and pointed towards her.

'You remind me of the babe.'

Kayla looked up and gasped. 'What babe?'

'The babe with the pink coffee cup,' Rick Deathsplash said.

He stared contemplatively at Kayla for a moment, then leaned an arm on Alonzo's shoulder and started to walk away.

'That was a crazy dream, man. I'll tell you about it sometime.'

'I'm the babe!' Kayla was still calling, as we were ushered out of the door.

Now that we were no longer bathed in the glow of Lacey Laine's dress, fame and beauty, people were much less willing to believe we were supposed to be there.

'I'm the babe! . . . *I'm* the babe!'

The door slammed shut, and she sighed.

Leroy walked up to her, ducking his head. 'If it helps, *I* think you're a babe.'

Kayla looked at him for a long moment. 'You were very good in there. The carrots were especially impressive.'

Looking up, Leroy gave a sheepish shrug. 'Well, I'm good under pressure. I just wanted to be a little help.'

'You were a *lot*tle help,' Kayla told him.

Freddie and I shared a look. Mine might have been a bit more of an eye-roll.

We made our way to Leroy's mum's car, where she was waiting with a picnic basket. I held my breath as I whipped Kayla's bag from the top of the trophy cup to find that Fluffy – for once – was exactly where he was supposed to be: curled up, taking a carroty nap.

Careful not to wake him, I put the goblet into the basket, and Leroy strapped down the lid.

'Guard this hamster with your life,' I warned Leroy, then looked between him and Freddie. Even if I hadn't been able to spend this week with Leo the way I'd planned to, I'd still been pretty lucky with the company I'd had. 'And thanks. Both of you. Are you sure you don't want to try and sneak in to watch the concert?'

Leroy shook his head rapidly. 'They're not really my speed.'

Freddie cast a nervous look at Kayla. 'Honestly . . . I think they're terrible. Sorry.'

I was still laughing about the look on her face as we

walked back across to the stadium – to the *real* entrance this time – and she hissed at me, 'I would *never* have let you date someone with such terrible taste.'

'He likes me!' I protested.

She sniffed, linking arms with me. 'Exactly.'

To my surprise, Mum was waiting for us outside.

'You'll have to ask your father about the VIP box,' she said, before I could even open my mouth. 'All I can tell you is it's nothing to do with me. But Jude was glad of a night out of the hotel, after the haunting.'

'You mean the technical malfunction?' I asked.

'And the giant black hamster that appears when someone's undone by their own pride,' Mum finished. Then she winked at me. 'Come on, then – let's find your dad.'

FORTY-SEVEN

Six days ago, Dad had been making us drive around Old Trafford while he scared old ladies and made up ridiculous rhyming chants. Now he was inside the stadium, in a special glass-fronted box with perfect views, its own private terrace of seats, and a buffet of finger sandwiches. I don't think he even cared that he wasn't there to watch football.

Walking through the VIP entrance felt like walking on the moon must have done to Neil Armstrong and Buzz Aldrin. Like stepping out into a place that had always seemed so beyond anything you were used to that reaching it seemed impossible.

I had to remember to take photos, otherwise I *knew* everyone back at school would say it was a hoax.

Only Jude didn't seem completely awed by the spectacle – he was most excited by the buffet he'd claimed a place in front of, watching cartoons on his iPad through noise-cancelling headphones.

'How did you *get this*?' I asked, while Dad beamed at me and Kayla like he'd just been officially appointed the new Santa Claus and had decided to go public with his secret identity.

'Tickets sold out in three minutes and nine seconds,' Kayla said, sliding open the glass doors and letting the crowd noise in with a whoosh. 'I was using two phones and all seven computers in the school library and hadn't got closer than four hundredth in the queue before they went.'

'They've been reselling on ticket sites for *thousands*.' I knew because I'd looked it up after Kayla lost the contest. When Dad lent me the money to upgrade my phone, I paid him back at ten pounds a month. If I'd asked him to buy us tickets for this, I'd have been repaying him for sixteen years.

'Lacey said it wasn't her,' Kayla said. 'So was it Rick? Was he paying me back for the coffee?'

'Or was it Jez? Is this a bribe so we won't mention how he tried to murder our hamster?'

Dad raised his hands to stop us talking, which was lucky because I was pretty sure we'd already run through the whole list of celebrities we sort-of knew. He folded his arms and tilted his head towards the entrance to the box.

'It wasn't any of those. It was *him*.'

In the doorway stood the hairy, slathering werewolf who'd been stalking us backstage. He was standing with his paws folded, looking as serious as a foam-and-

313

fur werewolf could.

Kayla blinked between me, Mum and Dad as if she'd missed some sort of joke. 'Are we supposed to know who this is?'

I was just staring at the wolf. Obviously I'd never seen the costume before tonight, but there was something about the pose. His height. How casual he looked in a ridiculous costume. There was only one person I knew who could carry off cool in a pair of paws.

'I think I might,' I said.

Dad grinned as I took a step towards the wolf at the door. Then another.

'Well fill us in, then,' Kayla said, confused. 'I didn't realize you were a dog person.'

I thought the puzzle pieces were slotting together in my head, but there was always a chance I'd be wrong. Still, saying them out loud made it feel more like it had to be true, so I started carefully. 'He had a last-minute dancing job. Just for this week.'

That made it click for Kayla too. I heard her gasp, but I didn't look her way.

I took another step towards the door.

'They needed someone with a specific kind of experience,' Mum said, nodding approvingly.

'And rehearsals meant we couldn't see each other for the whole of half-term. But Dad and Jude were going to be in Manchester anyway, and maybe there happened to be a space on Feet of the Future . . .'

'Someone always drops out of these things last minute,' Dad agreed.

'And you wanted to come to try out for that competition. I mean, Camp Cheer.'

Kayla shot a guilty look at my parents.

'We figured that out,' Mum said.

'Which meant we'd all be here. We just needed tickets.'

I finished closing the distance between me and the werewolf. He lowered his head slowly to my chest, and I reached out to tug at his tufty ears.

'Do they give dancers free tickets or something?' I asked, as the wolf head came loose in my hands.

Leo straightened up and laughed. 'Not ones this good. Rick's personal assistant Alonzo was meant to be up here, but he came in today and announced he couldn't let Rick out of his sight. He's watching from backstage instead. I don't know what got into him, but when I gave him your names for my guest list, he said he was upgrading you on the spot.'

'You planned this the *whole time*,' I whispered.

'I felt terrible about having to cancel,' Leo said, his voice soft enough that it sounded like his words were meant just for me. 'It's been ages since the summer, and

I've hardly seen you. I thought taking this job would mess everything up.'

It was so weird to hear Leo sounding as worried as I'd been this whole time. It was almost as if we felt exactly the same about each other.

'I've just caused a riot at a hotel and rescued a hamster from going up in smoke,' I told Leo. 'I'm basically the king of messing up. And I don't think you could ever, ever mess things up with me.'

'No need to thank me, by the way,' Dad was saying. 'No need to say *thanks*, Dad, for all the hours of planning this took. I just like seeing you happy, no thanks needed. Nope. None at all.'

Mum needled him in the ribs with a sharp elbow, grinning.

I smiled. 'Thanks, Dad,' I said, but most of the words were lost in the hug I was getting from my brilliant werewolf boyfriend.

Leo couldn't stay long. The concert had been delayed by him and Lacey pulling the power, but he had to get back down before he was needed onstage. Kayla and I headed out on to the balcony just as amazing, hamster-free fireworks went off across the stadium in bursts of silver and gold.

The concert was incredible. Rick Deathsplash screeched through his screamiest singles on the stage, and forty thousand people added their voices to his in a discordant, happy harmony. The high notes must have soared all the way across Manchester.

Leroy and Freddie video called just in time for the last song of the night, the one that the whole Ghoulish Games tour had been named after. Mum went to tell Jude the news that Fluffy was safe and nibbling his way through a hotel towel, while I held up the phone over my head like a torch to let them watch as we bounced to the music. Kayla was screaming Rick's name, but I couldn't look away from the dancers.

Well, maybe just one of them.

Dad had told me he'd planned for Leo to spend the whole weekend with us, exploring the city. I had ideas about that. I already knew the light-strewn, rainbow-painted street I wanted to go to the most.

As the concert came to a close with even more fireworks going off over Old Trafford – theatre of dreams and, for one night, home of Nightmares – and Rick Deathsplash pulled Lacey Laine out on to the stage to sing the last few lines just to her, I walked into the box to find a headless, panting werewolf back at the door.

I reached out and took the only hands I knew I wanted to hold, and Leo ducked his head to kiss me.

Kayla had been right when she'd said I had to

decide what was worth waiting for.

It had been *this*, all along.

There wasn't any substitute for love.

THE END

ABOUT THE AUTHOR

Before writing her first novel, Birdie dabbled in the theatre, sold books at Waterstones, ran drama classes for children, and dispensed romantic advice to internet daters. She studied at two universities cunningly disguised as stately homes, taking a BA in Creative and Professional Writing at St Mary's, Twickenham, and an MA in Writing for Young People at Bath Spa, where she gained first-class degrees in between looking for secret passageways and dodging peacocks.

Birdie is pro body positivity and anti bullying, and believes in kindness above all things. She lives in Surrey, where she writes despite the best interruptive efforts of her pets, Ziggy Starcat and Moppet the Wonder Dog.

ACKNOWLEDGEMENTS

Getting to the thank yous happens to be one of my favourite parts of writing a book. Not only because it confirms that the book is done and you've somehow managed to put several thousand words in a reasonably sense-making sort of order, but because it's a very good reminder that no one does it alone.

So I firstly need to thank the marvellous people at my publisher: my editors, Venetia and George, plus Amber, Simran and the whole team. A huge thank you to Linzie Hunter for another fantastic cover.

Thank you to my agent, Molly Ker Hawn, always, for her wit and wisdom, Alywn Hamilton for calm words and pre-book launch survival tips, and Sophie Cameron and Simon James Green for their support.

Thanks to the Bath Spa gang, who I promise to see more of, and to all my brilliant friends who are always there for me, whether it's on a six-hour drive to a random tiny village, or in the front row of the world's most baffling rock musical.

Thank you to Hannah Love for a ridiculous number of things, and to my cousins, Talia and Katy W, for knowing I needed you before I did. I wish we were in a less rubbish club, but at least the company is good.

Thank you to my cousin Rachael, an exceptionally good human, for all the phone check-ins and the war horse.

Thank you to Keely, Mici, Carlee and New York for making me smile when I really needed to.

I'd also like to thank David Bowie, Prince, Brian Harvey and Matt Damon, who have all contributed indirectly to this book by way of inspiration, and any readers who've spotted exactly where and how (we can be friends).

And Robbie Savage, That Peter Crouch Podcast, Mollie and Rosie Kmita, Fighting Talk, Chris Sutton and Alistair Bruce-Ball for making me laugh about football.

And of course thanks to my dad, who I'll trick into reading one of my books one day, and to my mum, accidental composer of all my best comedy lines, who I miss every moment, and who I'll always write all of them for.

NEED SOME SUPPORT?

If you have some questions, or just want to learn more about issues related to being LGBTQ+, you might like to get in touch with one of the support organisations below.

The Proud Trust
www.theproudtrust.org

Young Stonewall
www.youngstonewall.org.uk
Visit their website to find out about their Rainbow
Laces campaign – *Making Sport Everyone's Game*

FFLAG
Families and Friends of Lesbians and Gays
www.fflag.org.uk